MILK-BLOOD

By
Mark Matthews

Thank Chris!

Mark Matthews

Wicked Run Press

PRAISE FOR MILK-BLOOD

"The originality and tension of the urban horror story, Milk-Blood is evident on every page. Matthews takes you to some very dark places, twists and turns, with the rabbit hole going deeper and deeper, until there is no way out. Not for the faint of heart, this story of love, loss, family and acceptance is a rollercoaster ride from start to finish." — *Richard Thomas, author of Staring Into the Abyss*

"What a dark, twisted and bizarre book this was. One of the most striking urban horror stories I have read in a long time." —Author Adam Light

"An incredibly powerful story and one of the most original horror novels I have read in years. Guaranteed to have you on the edge of your seat!" —*The Horror Bookshelf*

"This is a helluva story. A discomforting tale of true inner city horrors, told by characters so real they pop off the page. Add the supernatural mix to the story and it really grabs you by the throat. Very much recommended!"
— *John F.D. Taff, author of Little Deaths*

ALSO BY THE AUTHOR

ON THE LIPS OF CHILDREN
"One of the scariest novels I've read all year." ~*The Horror News Network*

STRAY
"Wildly empathic. Stray sings!" ~*Sacha Z. Scoblic, author of Unwasted: My Lush Sobriety*

Wicked Run Press

Cover design by Elderlemon Design
Edited by Richard Thomas

Copyright © Mark Matthews and Wicked Run Press, 2014
ISBN-13 978-0692207956
ISBN-10 0692207953

"Ultimately all of us are alone in the universe — the only person we ever really know deeply is ourselves. Obviously, I've never been a dwarf or a princess, so when I'm writing these characters I have to try and get inside their skin and see what the world would be like from their position. It's not always easy." -George RR Martin

<u>MILK-BLOOD</u>: *The act of extracting heroin-laden blood for reinjection at a later time. It usually is one's own blood, but could also be the blood of someone who has just overdosed. It is done as insurance in case one's heroin supply runs out. The term is used in Neil Young's 'The Needle and the Damage Done': "milk-blood to keep from running out."*

Milk-Blood

By Mark Matthews

* IMPORTANT NOTE FROM THE AUTHOR

The story you are about to read is entirely true. I know there was a disclaimer that called this a piece of fiction and that any resemblance to an actual person, living or dead, is entirely coincidental. It has to say that. So now if you are damaged while reading the story, I am no longer liable.

I am the author of three novels as well as a social worker and a therapist. Exposure to such a myriad of human experience provides fodder for writing material, but my ideas for novels come at me from all angles. The ones that seem to stick are those summoned not just from individuals I meet, but from settings. Setting radiates energy into the air. Every place has its own music if you listen, and I try to hear it and capture it. That's how my first three novels came forth.

This story you are reading relied on a place I was able to easily summon into my brain. I invited the characters who lived there into my heart so I could write from theirs.

Where is this?

Detroit. On a specific urban street called Brentwood where magnificent, ancient houses that once gleamed with pride have begun to crumble. A neighborhood where if you have fresh tags on your license plates you have to bring them inside or else they may be stolen. Where if you bring a new TV into your house it will get ripped off soon enough, for watchful eyes are everywhere. Where families fear letting their kids on the street not just for the street thugs, but for the stray dogs.

I have visited families on downtrodden streets of Detroit as a social worker more than once. One family is easily summoned from my memory, partly due to the burned down house next door to them. The burns were fresh, it seemed, since you could see where the flames had been flickering out the windows and charbroiled burnt marks remained. It was one of many abandoned houses that would at best be boarded up, but never demolished.

My client was a mother who lived with her teenage son and the rotting remains of the house next door were just part of their problems. My job as a therapist was to stop the family decay and help the family stay intact. Many words were said during our in-home therapy session, but the ones that stick with me were said by the mother. "I wish he would be more grateful, I should have had an abortion."

These words were terrible for the son to hear, but I did my best to open my soul to all her life experiences that lead up to this statement. "Advanced accurate empathy" is the clinical term for the ability to infer the thoughts and feelings of another, and to put oneself in their internal world and perceptions.

At that moment, I felt an onslaught of heat, like the flames from next door were still flickering and came into me. The feelings from these flames guide me as I write each and every word that follows from here.

Chapter One: Zachary - *10 am, Day after Christmas*

Puddles of mud.

After she confessed her eyes became puddles of mud, like tears had fallen upon dirty eye sockets and left a muddy mess.

"Okay, yes, it was Puckett. We had sex," she squeaked. "Three times only. I didn't mean to. Will you still take care of us?"

Latrice only confessed because she was caught. The paternity test showed a 99 percent chance that Zach wasn't the father. She held the child of Puckett in her womb.

"Will you take care of us?" she asked again. It wasn't a question. She was giving him a challenge. He took care of what he loved. His mother had been his to tend to for years, and they both got by with the help of some pills. He would take care of her until one of them died, because that's what he did. But Latrice with another man's child inside of her?

"I will take care of things," he answered, but he didn't say the rest that he wanted to, which was, "*Because the day I fucked you I caught an infection and now I have it for life.*"

"What about Puckett? Will you do him like you usually do?"

"Yes, I will."

He had to. Because now Puckett has the infection too, and he was sure to come around running his mouth about being the father of Latrice's child.

Puckett spent three more days alive before Zach found him. Suffocation by choking had always been his choice when he wanted others to think for a moment about whose hands were killing them. His hands came alive with power when wrapped around someone's throat. Like squeezing a loaf of soft bread he could squeeze necks, but when his hands were around Puckett's bulging windpipe, he eased up. He wanted to hear him talk. He wanted a confession. When one didn't come and Puckett played stupid, he squeezed until he saw a shade of blue in Puckett's face and his body danced on the edge of death. Then he relaxed his fingers and let him gasp for air and come back to life. Dipping him in, and pulling him out. He could have done it all day, and nearly did, until the shade of blue seemed to burst and no more air was needed.

Later, Puckett would swim deep. The Detroit River doesn't give up its dead easy, and it was a better option than his burn and bury method. Last time he burned something was when he fire-bombed the house across the street with a Molotov cocktail made of vodka (100 proof). The whole block around Brentwood was rained on with ashes and soot of the boy who died that night. Latrice loved it when she could get into his head and make him kill, except for this time when a boy had died. But now she was giving birth to a new child, a baby girl, to replace him on this street. Spirit in, spirit out.

Labor pains doubled her over in pain a month before her due date, and Zach drove her to the hospital at 4:30 am on a Tuesday. The delivery room was lit like a spaceship and reminded Zach of his trip to Vegas. No windows, no escape, and you won't leave without being changed. He couldn't tell if it was day or night as the hours passed. He slipped out more than once to chew on his own supply of Percocets or Vicodins or Xanax, and came back feeling cleansed each time.

What he saw was a foreign liquid flowing from between Latrice's propped up legs. It smelled of something spoiled being cooked, something ominous—bigger than her, bigger than this hospital could handle. Latrice went inward into silent agony at times, at other times yelled not with words but noises. She dripped sweat, spasmed, and when the head crowned, Zach felt both nauseous bile and warm shivers of hope.

There was a one percent chance that the baby girl would have his ebony flesh. The miracle waited in his chest, thumping, wanting to explode. But on first sight the thump died. She did not. In fact, the baby's flesh was a veiny blue color and so pale it was nearly see-through.

A heart condition kept the child in intensive care for days, in an incubator, looking like a blue frog ready to be dissected. Zach peeked in at her and tried to make eye contact, did make eye contact. This infant seemed to be his very own heart beating in front of him, shriveled and alien, with doctors prodding it to keep it alive.

"She's going to die," Latrice repeated again and again. "I can't take this, I can't see her. You do it, you stay here."

He did, and he slept in the hospital on plastic pillows while Latrice went home to watch over his mother who lived with them on 618 Brentwood Drive.

His lone finger in the sterile glove touched the infant girl's forehead.

Where's my mother? She asked him with tiny motions of her incubated arms.

Soon. Soon you will see her. I am here. This is how it is.

Days later, talking hospital heads gave him instructions and medicine and appointment reminders, and he brought the child home to Latrice. Life had grown stronger in the nameless infant, but she was still barely bigger than the palm of his hand. At home the child shrieked and wailed as if it hurt just to be alive.

"This is not how it's supposed to be," Latrice said, watching Zach holding the wailing child at 3:36 am in the rocker on a Tuesday.

"This is how it's going to be."

He slept with the 10 day old baby flesh on his own. The skin was so thin you could see her insides, like it wasn't fully done growing and she was thrown into the world before her time. Their bodies warmed each other and he rocked her on his chest until 4:25 am. She fell asleep against the beat of his heart.

On her mother's chest, she refused to take the breast and would not sup at the nipple introduced to her mouth. Latrice seemed as scared of the child as the child was of it.

Medications the baby did take. Zach injected them into an IV port in her neck. Warnings from doctors rang in his ears. Too large of an injection could lead to asphyxiation. Failure to administer would do the same. She was already like so many who lived on this street and needed a daily drug to face each day.

Latrice curled up into a ball much of the time. Her hair, unwashed for days, became stringy as a broom. Pill bottles with the prescription labels rubbed off sat on the counter. Oxys or Xanax or both.

The infant tears came at night—sometimes for hours, non-stop. When they got too much and it seemed the child herself might shatter, the parents would wrap themselves in jackets against the cold and take dark trips to the hospital, only to be sent back home again. Sleeplessness weighed them down like soaking wet clothes.

"This isn't how it's supposed to be," she said.

"This is how it is," he answered.

"No. No. You can take care of this. Take care of her like you do. Make it like it was before. She's not meant to be alive." Her eyes filled with tears once again. They pleaded to him. The infection bubbled in his veins.

Killing again would be easy.

He walked around the house, pacing, gaining energy with each stride, summoning up the courage to do the deed. This one needed to be fast and clean, unlike Puckett.

When he held the pillow over her face, he smothered her with his whole body weight to make it quick, but it may not have been needed. Things were fragile already, and they were just tiny breaths to take away this time.

The body fit easily into his trunk, the night air cold around him. The car seats were frigid leather. Soon the car would heat up, and things would be better. He whispered middle of the night words to his passenger in the back seat.

"We're taking mommy to her grave. Then we'll be home, and I will give you a name, and I will take care of you as long as I live."

My infection is gone, he thought, as he drove with the body ready to burn and bury.

FROM THE AUTHOR - As both a social worker and a writer, I have always believed in the adage that everyone is the hero of their own story. None of us view ourselves as an evil-doer. If there is evil being done, it is for revenge or it is justified based on a hurt done to us. So I write the same scene from inside the head of Latrice.

Chapter Two: Latrice - *10 am, Day after Christmas*

Fluid filled her eyes and burned like acid. It gathered in her eye sockets and sizzled the color right off of her pupils before spilling over the side. Big teardrops rolled down her cheeks.

This was all wrong. All of it was wrong and her gut hurt so bad she wondered if the baby would be vomited right out of her.

The baby was causing this pain. It grew in her like an ulcer.

"Puckett," she said. "It was Puckett."

The words felt good to say. She blamed Puckett. She knew he hated Puckett, she knew he would believe it was Puckett, and she knew he would kill Puckett like he had killed for her before.

The first killing was her stepfather. Shot him in the head and then burned and buried both the gun and the body. Since that time, it was like she was set free. Like her prince had kissed her cheek and woke her up. Now she was connected to Zach forever. She was in his skin. She was in his blood. When they fucked, she left part of her own spirit in his bloodstream. She was quite sure his veins were lined with parts of her. Sometimes Zack hated that but she knew it gave him purpose. Without her to serve what would he do? Without lives to take, what would his own life mean? Nothing. Nothing at all.

Making people her puppets is what she was good at. She'd been getting in peoples' heads her whole life.

Zach had fire in his eyes for Puckett now, and Puckett deserved to die slowly for a million crimes, but his seed had never been inside of her, and he certainly wasn't there when she was walking by 617 Brentwood Street.

617 Brentwood was now nearly destroyed, bombed out by Zach who fucked the job up being wrecked on Xanax and vodka. It was messy. His target was someone else, but the man was not home, only the man's son was there. Left alone at 8 years old. She hated to think about it. She looked at the rotting timbers of the house sliding and disintegrating into the earth, day by day, and she had to do some quick self-surgery on her psyche.

A tragedy. Who would do such a thing? I am glad it was someone else, and not the man I am with.

It wasn't hard to distance herself when she looked at the blackened embers.

Why didn't she move from this street?

Because families stay here forever. You don't get out of here. Everyone on this street is related. Somebody in a house dies, a relative scoops the house up, pays some taxes on it, and invites the other half of the family over to stay.

Seeing the charred remains of the house was like seeing the insides of someone's body. Like their skin was tore off and just the guts and skeleton were left. It looked ugly. The front window seemed like a mouth, and the big dormer window on the second story was the eye that looked over the whole street. Now the eye was blotted out and the glass was broken. The white was charcoal black. Bars on the windows remained and it looked like a vacant jail cell. The front porch had started to sink.

Xanax and liquor put Zach into a raging blackout, but somehow he passed the police interview two days later. Stuffed animals and balloons had been placed on the front lawn by grieving neighbors for a week or so, but they became dirty, forgotten, and now were long gone.

The kid didn't burn, the smoke killed him, she told herself. Whoever did this, was an evil man, but it wasn't her Zach.

She forced the thoughts from her skull and was ready to move on when she saw a light brown boot in the overgrown grass. She tracked the boot up and saw the leg inside a pair of dirty jeans.

Dead or alive? Was her first question. Alive was her quick answer, since a dead body would have been hidden deeper in the grass, like the last one they found here stuck under some trash. If it was buried nobody would have bothered.

This brown boot was either part of a sleeping street person or just some wasted fuck. She needed to walk by. She was carrying a plastic grocery bag with five packages of Ramen noodles, a quart of milk, and some lucky charms. The milk made the bag way too heavy. Why do they always ask if she wants her milk in a bag? Like they are too lazy to put the damn thing in the bag themselves.

She could feel the plastic stretching, slipping, ready to break. She moved her fingers for a better grip but needed to get home before the bag burst and everything splattered.

But something stopped her. The body. She had to look. She took a few steps closer.

No, he wasn't moving. Maybe he was dead.

She nudged his boot slightly with the edge of her foot, and it swayed one way and then back. Her eyes traveled up his body to his arm and figured out what had happened. A needle was sticking into his underarm liked he'd been hit by an arrow, and something was tied around his bicep.

Shadows from overgrown grass gave much of the body cover, but the skin she could see was a dark black and a shade deeper than hers even. She waited to sense for motions. His boot remained still, his chest seemed stationary. He was not living. Or perhaps this was the sleep of the overdosed, the coma of the high, and he had nodded out right there but would soon emerge.

She tightened her grip on the plastic bag, took a step forward to move on, and then heard a rustle in the grass.

Her head turned, she took another step, and then she felt it. Clutching onto her ankle. It was the grip of his hand.

She tried to kick her leg forward and pull free but could not. The clutch was strong and full of life. Long fingers squashed her bone the harder she pulled. She tugged with her whole body and dropped the bag of groceries. The milk hit the ground and burst.

A second hand grasped her leg and pulled her to the ground. She landed with a thump and he hovered over her. The smell was rotten. His skin was dark, crispy, and mixed with the reddish scabs that weren't bleeding but the color of blood. The whites of his eyes were huge. He had no eyebrows or eyelashes.

She'd fought off tweaking crackheads before, but this creature was strong and mentally ill. She could feel the power of his sickness. She screamed, gained power, and freed one leg to kick at the man's face. *Smack*, she made contact, like kicking a soccer ball. His head jerked back.

But he was not fazed and was back on top of her. His smell penetrated and filled her lungs. She beat on the man's chest and felt it thump like it was hollow. Just the whites of his eyes shined in the dusky air under a street full of broken street lights.

"You," his voice spoke with rotten breath. "You will like a little piece of me. You'll see. Just a little shot of me."

She fought back but her arms felt frail as a child.

With one hand he grabbed the needle from his arm. It was stuck there like a dart that needed to be tugged out of cork. The needle came free and he held it in front of his eyes. Traces of a liquid dripped from the tip. In an instant he smashed the needle into his own chest. *Thwack,* and his body pulsated with energy. He began to draw from the syringe, slowly, like what was coming out from his chest was too thick to fit through the needle.

She fumbled on the ground for something to fight with. Tiny rocks, pebbles between her fingers, nothing that could help. The milk puddled under her head and made her hair wet. The milk was still cold. She remembered that. And she remembered how warm his body felt on top of her. Feverish.

"You'll always be a part of me..."

He stabbed the needle into her groin. The hard, thick metal made her gasp like she had been impaled through her slit up her spine. Time seemed to stop, and everything was motionless. The sky above was the dark blue of dusk and a fluff of cloud looked down. She laid there like she was six years old and gazed up, hoping the ice cream man would brave her street and she'd hear the sweet jingle of the white truck.

The needle had impaled her, crucified her, and something pulsed inside. She was being filled with all the dirt and grime of the gutter of this street. All the discarded waste of dying skin and lost hopes and crumbling walls and peeling paint and broken 40 ounce glass and tweaking crack head nerves filled her insides.

She woke in her bed.

How she got there she was not sure.

Days that followed were not the same. A pit of despair expanded in her stomach. She imagined it like a peach pit, hard and shriveled, but this one grew. Despite not taking care of herself, it grew. At times it would kick, often it would make her puke, and she imagined the substance that came up was the result of a miscarriage. Her body was discarding the poison.

When she got the ultrasound and they rubbed the cold gel on her belly and found a heartbeat, only then did she believe it was human. It was not waiting to be born, but waiting to come and get her.

The hospital that day was the dusk of a night she didn't want to face. Even the clean, well-lit hospital felt dirty. Spasms stretched her muscles and pain came in unrelenting waves. She needed the evil out of her. The nurses came and went and wrote their name with a blue marker on the dry erase board in her room. Medical equipment stood guard and waited.

Zach was there and spoke but she pretended he wasn't. She wanted some dope, some Oxy, she wanted an epidural stuck inside her forever. If she could have reached, she would have grabbed something sharp to cut her own veins and take the pain away.

When the child was out of her, she felt such relief. The baby was barely human and still a tiny fetus. Its skin was blue and translucent from a "cyanotic" heart defect. It was defective, she already knew that, and here it would die. Time to go home and leave the defective baby at the hospital.

She went home, but Zach remained.

Days at home alone and she felt cold and hollow. Zach's mom was home too but Latrice paid her little mind and the new grandmother was barely fed.

Latrice wore sweaters on top of shirts and pulled the sleeves over her hands. She wasn't sure when to change, wasn't sure if she ate. Xanax become her vitamins. Each quiet moment was just waiting to be shattered by a phone call from Zach saying that the baby had died, that the infant wasn't fit to live. Instead, every call from Zach was asking how his mom was doing and if the house was ready for the baby to come home. Latrice said little, and what she did say was muttered without conviction.

When Zach finally carried the tiny infant through the door, Latrice looked down at the creature for the first time. Breathing on its own, outside of an incubator, and part of her family. *Maybe this will spark something in me,* she hoped, *maybe looking in her eyes will change things.*

But the baby's skin was still blue, like she was amphibious. It was like you could see the rotting wood of her insides ready to crumble if held the wrong way. Eyes were bulged. Skin was soft but wrinkly. One large hand could squeeze and crush her to death in an instant.

The first night was quiet and easy.

The second night, the infant's tears cut into her eardrums. It went on day and night, each time stopping only long enough to tease her hopes that the quiet would persist. The infant's high-pitched wails became the background of her life. Especially at night in the darkness it shattered her sleep. The Xanax and Oxys were like cotton cushions for her ears. Glances from Zach burned her with disdain while he tried to comfort the baby. Trips to the hospital in the middle of the night happened more than once, and she prayed the doctors would say, *This is serious, we better keep her here,* " but it never happened. Instead, they stayed in ERs with glances from others and drove home with the same infant.

"It's not supposed to be like this," she told Zach.

"This is how it is," he forced back.

"No. You can take care of this. Take care of her like you do. Make it like it was before. She's not meant to be alive."

She saw the shift in his eyes. She had convinced him, and he would kill for her again. He was going to put to sleep for good the horrible child she created. The aching in her gut that never left no matter how many pills she took would probably live on, but maybe it would fade and decompose with the child's body.

She heard him leave the room with purpose to take care of the child. His feet were heavy with his years. She closed her eyes and curled up into a tiny ball, tight as she could. The inside of her eyelids weren't as dark as she wanted them to be so she pulled the covers over her head. But then she heard the footsteps return. He was back. She pulled the covers down and rolled her body to face him, and saw the whites of his eyes hovering above.

Then the pillow smothered her face, pressed against her mouth with Zach's full weight.

She was the one being put to sleep.

Brought to life by the fear of death, her body burned with a new strength. She reached up for his arms and scratched, grabbed, and beat on anything she could. Nothing let up. His arms were taut and thick like a piece of firewood. She tried to murmur something but there was no room for words or screams.

A burning started inside of her where her lungs ached for air. Her head got fuzzy. She saw visions of Zach raising this child on his own. Both of them were smiling, both were monsters. This was his plan all along, to make her have this baby and then get rid of her. All she could do was scream on the inside with her lungs on fire.

You and this child will not live in peace. I will come for her.

The beating of her heart was so loud she was sure it would be heard by neighbors and they would save her. This couldn't be the end. Something had to happen.

It did not. The last heartbeats of her life were the most rapid, powerful ones she had in all of her 26 years. Her brain went dead, her heart stopped beating, blood no longer passed through her veins, but the fire inside burned eternal.

Chapter Three: Zach Talks to the Detectives

Lilly's tiny body was held up against his chest and her head rested on the top of his shoulder. With one large hand on her back held firm he was able to move about the house. He was making his mom a grilled cheese and tomato soup, but the damn soup splattered in the microwave and the grilled cheese got so dark he might have to start over. It made him dash about the kitchen, and the milk in Lilly's stomach was surely swirling about.

Don't puke, damn it, stay down.

She'd drunk half the bottle, which was more than usual, and he was just waiting for the vomit to come up. Each bottle she took this week has been followed by sticky and warm goop out of her mouth, like some bird shit, and it ended up all over his back.

He was sure she could feel his chest vibrate with anger whenever this happened. This baby had become part of his own heartbeat, and her milky spit up began to coat his life. It would end up on her bib, her blankets, on the bed sheets, and dribbling down her chin. He got used to its smell everywhere. It was the stink of her sickened insides.

But she needed to be fed and grow. She needed to get smart and fast. He couldn't keep this up forever. He needed for her brain to grow inside that shrunken skull of hers.

And the way her skin was, it seemed all of her organs could be seen by everyone. Hospital doctors called it cyanosis. They talked about surgery and survival rates. They explained it with low confidence but in high terms, talked with their hands, and went on as long as they needed to until everyone was bored and confused enough not to ask any more questions.

The words mixed in with those of geriatric doctors who rambled on about his mom's blood thinners and diabetes and wound vacs, until all of it was a sloppy mix of medical jargon and the two women had become one big patient.

Zac was the one keeping both of them alive. You don't put down a child's mom without taking care of the child, that was a code he felt inside that was impossible to break. If Lilly's heart stopped beating, so would his own. And you take care of your own mother, best you can with what you got. Now he had one baby in the crib, and the other woman on the couch, both needing to be fed. Easy the first of the month when Mamma's check comes and food stamp money renews, but some days best he can do is not enough.

Zach had just succeeded in chopping off the crusts of the grilled cheese, making it into squares of four, when there was a knock at the door. He knew from instinct it was a detective knock. Or a cop's knock. Or Protective Service or someone with a badge and uniform. There were badges behind that rap.

He didn't answer, so harder detective knocks came. Meal's gonna get cold, he thought, and his momma would have to wait on the couch. He tried to hurry, and the sharp ridges of the food-pantry soup can top cut into his skin, right on the edge of drawing blood, but none came forth.

Never look down and to the left. Then they know you are lying. And never give anything up. Never give anything up. Mutter "lawyer" if you have to. And expect tricks. They will rephrase your words into something different and see if you agree to a different version. They will say they have an eyewitness. They will try to be your friend and say, "I am just like you. I understand why you did it, she deserved it." These guys get off on confessions like it's their smack. They sneak into your head and make you say shit and do shit and laugh to their family about you when they go home.

Lilly was like a kangaroo cub nestled in the pouch of his hand when he opened the front door and saw the cops. Plain clothes cops. Or detectives, either way. One black, one white, and two more officers in a squad car on the street with the blue lights on. The lights flashed and spun, flashed and spun, hitting the house again and again, and were just part of the cop's power play. His brother Nelson next door, who was too chicken shit to help take care of their mom, had certainly seen the squad cars by now as well.

"We doing this once more?" Zach asked before they could speak. Lilly kept facing her head in different directions against his shoulder.

"We will come back until she's found," the cop answered. "I know you want that."

"So you say. You get out there and find her then."

"It's what we have been doing. And we know you have been too. We just need more information from you. We will work together. We know you want to find her."

"For sure I do. I can't do this on my own. We all need her here. If she wants to, we are here waiting."

"Then you need to tell us again when you saw her last. Maybe you remember something else. Then we can help. You mind if we come in?" The white cop feigned manners, and Zach remembered him. He was here a month ago for the search warrant with disdain in his eyes and a cocky walk. Today they sent a new black guy with him. Guy was young and wouldn't lock eyes with Zach at all costs. Zach saw that.

"You want me to lie? You tell your own lies like you want. This is my truth. And I told you, we had a fight, I went to bed, then she was gone. She's with that man Jeremiah Puckett, I know it."

"It's the Puckett family who say different," the white cop said as the black one took a step inside. Zach squeezed tighter onto Lilly and let go of the door. "We might not even be here just for your woman missing. Figured she would leave you. That we might believe. Maybe that girl you're holding wants her momma back, but nobody else does. But the Puckett family…they got friends."

"I already talked about all of this and that junkie ass Puckett. They recorded me. You heard it. But you want to keep coming to see me, go ahead come on in." Zach stepped back and felt his skin start to itch. He sniveled in some mucus, felt sweat. He hadn't had a bit of his own Vicodin in hours.

The cops took a step in and their eyes scanned the place. One gave a nod to Zach's mom who was on the couch. She didn't nod back, but her mouth chomped, like a horse, always moistening her mouth and her lips. Swallowing was getting harder for her. Someday he'd have to suction it up they said.

"Look, we aren't accusing you of anything. We aren't going there," the cop who had been silent finally spoke. "Just tell us more so we can find out what happened after your fight. And... " he paused as if waiting to see if Zach would speak, "we got a guy who saw you with her after that night you say she went missing, a guy who says he will testify you were angry if he has to. We thought that was odd he'd lie on you like that."

Zach adjusted Lilly in his arms. There had been no vomit. The formula she took down had stayed in her gut. Like him, she learned to keep shit in her mouth and not puke up at the wrong time when a cop was in your face.

"You got a guy, huh? Everybody's got a guy. You got a guy like that then I'm in cuffs. So be it. I got a girl. Two of them. I got to go. I got my momma who's hungry and my daughter in my hands. You think I don't want you to find her and to help take care of my momma and this sick little kid? My momma's starting to forget things and will need diapers soon as this girl needs none. And this baby girl goes to the hospital every few days. You want to arrest me. Again. You get me a fuckin nanny to take care of them. Go ahead, I need a break."

"Could be you just enjoy getting your mother's check. We know you are her payee each month. And I can arrest you for something easy. We can get a warrant to search your mother's ass, you know that."

"And I know y'all will. You will enjoy that shit. Now happy holidays, and be gone."

Zach could hear his momma's breathing change from the couch. He grabbed the door as if to swing it closed, but just then the black cop stuck his finger towards Lilly's chest. He placed it inside Lilly's tiny palm like he was some politician. Before Zach could pull away, Lilly grasped it, as if a finger in her hand was new.

"And don't think child protective service is done yet."

Child protective service. CPS was worse than cops.

Child protective service workers were just angry women trying to fuck with his life. They already had a CPS woman come to the house to look inside each cupboard. They made Zach get a new crib that didn't have side-sliding gates. They talked to him like he was a child and warned him about heating up formula in a microwave and to swear he never would. Made him show where he would keep the medications locked. He had to get new screens upstairs. He had to sign a release so the woman could talk to Lilly's doctors and confirm she was going to her appointments and getting treated for her heart defect. All of that, and she still wrote in her report that he may not be capable of taking care of an old woman and a young infant at the same time.

The cop poked his fingers at Lilly like they were family. Zach waited, patient, felt like a dog getting its ass sniffed, but had nearly had enough. The man finally pulled his finger away.

"If you ask me, this ain't barely even a child. Some kind of alien. What is this damn blue thing anyways?"

Zach's chest beat in anger. Lilly was held up against it, and her own leaking heart certainly felt the thump.

"You know anything sweet pea?" The cop asked as if Lilly could understand. "What do you know about your mommy? If you could talk, you would tell us everything. Maybe someday you will."

The cop looked up into Zach's eyes, felt the burn of his gaze, but didn't back down. "If she could talk, she would tell us everything, because she wants you gone to prison," he said. "She knows you can't take care of her."

If Zach's hands were free of the child, he would have taken a swing. A right hook to his cheek would knock him off guard, and then a barrage of punches would follow. But the child in his arms stopped all of this, and he kept his mouth shut and his fist unclenched. His unreleased tension seethed throughout the room, the temperature climbed, his nerves vibrated.

The moment was interrupted by the smacking of his mom's tongue. She was listening from the couch, wetting her lips, and about to speak.

"You men. You two all up in here while your people across the street doing the real work. They talking to that sad homeless man right now, the real menace of this street. He's no good. He knows things. Go outside, sure enough, you'll see them. You'll find everything you need from the man across the street if you just ask him in the right voice. No need to scare a tiny child before she knows she should be scared of you two. Please go, I'm sick and tired."

Lilly started to squirm as if she was listening to her Grandma speak. Zach positioned her so that her head was looking over his shoulder, and then he felt a gas bubble come up her chest and vomit came out of her mouth. Warm spit-up was on his back.

"We'll try another time ma'am," one cop responded. "I know we all want what's best."

Zach patted Lilly's back and watched the cops walk out the door. It was clear he had won this round, but the victory wasn't complete until they drove off. Instead, they wandered across the street with guns and cuffs blazing on their belts. They were off to join the other two cops who were talking to the crazy homeless man, just like his momma said. Four cops, all waving their flashlights and walking in circles like it was a crime scene, not looking for clues—looking for a crime.

Zach knew the squatter was too crazy to say much. He'd heard the man blabbing to himself before like he was at church speaking in tongues. The man was frantically checking his pockets, waving his hands in the air, and certainly the cops would tire of this. Zach closed the door and let them be.

"How did you know what was going on out there, Ma?"

"Those men," his mom said, and smacked her lips, "what do they know? Don't know this street like I do. Like you do. I know what time it is. I know when there's a woman getting beat on three doors down at the Bloomers, or when Ronnie Harris is back in lock-up. We got that power to know. You got that power. I know what you do. Doesn't mean I'm no witch like they say. Just means we watch and feel. We know check dates. We know the weather. We know who got tires stolen by how cars set up on the bricks. Don't need a badge for that. Know how to make money off suburban kids looking for the crack rocks like you do. Know when to duck and take care of business."

Mom's eyes looked around the room like she was talking to spirits and not to her son. Some day she wouldn't even know my name, Zach thought. He knew this day was coming.

"They don't know shit, Ma, you are right about that."

And Lilly didn't know anything either, and wouldn't say anything if she could talk.

She'd never know that the same hand that patted her back softly to cough up the milky vomit had held down a pillow over her mother's face until she died. These hands also burned the body with gas, dug a hole, buried the body with fertilizer, chopped at it with the shovel, and covered it up.

The police did come back the next day to search the home with another warrant. They sifted through the cereal boxes, through Grandma's old makeup, through her incontinence supplies. They found one mostly smoked joint. No guns, no bodies, no blood of Latrice on anything, just an expired license plate on Zach's car. They should have searched the house across the street, about three feet under the ground in the back yard. The homeless riff raff who littered the lawn of the burnt out house were sitting on Lilly's momma. Zach had returned her to the home he exploded with a firebomb made of vodka. He buried her there.

FROM THE AUTHOR - Ten years pass, and now Lilly is old enough for her own chapter. After much deliberation, I've decided to switch from the 3rd person to the 1st person point of view for Lilly's portion of this story. Something inside says it's the right thing to do, and this story suddenly becomes more personal to her plight.

Chapter Four: Lilly's First Day in Sixth Grade

I felt the acid bubble up my throat. They called it heartburn, and my heart always seemed to be burning. Something hot and fiery was trickling up from my belly and tearing up my insides. Once in a while, it dripped into my lungs and I coughed it up. Then I'd have to find a place to spit and it felt like a hot peach pit. But most times I couldn't cough hard enough and it would drip back deeper into me.

I wanted the burning to stop for good. I wanted someone to tell me how not to feel on fire like this. That was all I wanted—for the fire to go out, and for someone to reach in and rip out my defective heart and leave a new one in its place. Fix my stomach and fix my heart. I don't even care if they leave another big scar.

I ate both breakfast and lunch at school, and it was full of lots of bread to soak up the molten lava inside. Breakfast was cheerios and a banana. Lunch was a turkey 'crows aunt'. Home tonight maybe we'd have day old donuts. If not, then Spaghettios which I would eat straight out of the can. I liked them going down cold.

Sometimes the hurt inside would make me want to cry, but not at school. You can't cry at school if there was no reason. Especially on your first day of school since they closed down the elementary you were supposed to go to and now you're in another first day at some strange place. Besides, I was pretty sure if I cried the tears would come out looking red and bloody.

I sat with my legs pulled into me and my arms wrapped around them, my back pressed up against the brick wall of the school. In front of me, sweaty boys played basketball. They rolled up their blue uniform shirts, pretended that they came untucked by accident, and smashed into each other. On the other side of the blacktop, the rhythmic slaps of jump ropes struck the pavement. Three tetherball sets stood all in a line. Two of them had no balls attached to the ropes, and the other one was being played with by children who were unsure of the rules.

Swings swayed back and forth, like a clock, tick-tock. The metal chain of one swing had been wrapped around the top cross pole and I wondered whose job it was to go up there and get it down. Maybe nobody. Maybe it just stayed up there until they closed this school too and I got shipped off to a new one.

The only kids that I knew who went to this school were younger than me. Ciara and Ciana lived four doors down and were drawing with chalk right now. They would let me join them, but if I played with them it would look desperate. When you look like I do, people either pulled you to their side to make you cool, or tried to make themselves cool by beating you down. I waited to see which way they'd treat me. Until then, they were just a group of kids, and I sat and watched.

I felt a ray of heat on my skin from someone's gaze, and looked up to see where it was from. Boys were glancing at me and nodding their heads in my direction. Secret words were being spoken. They saw me look and came over to stand before me. I pulled my legs tighter into my chest and they were towering over me.

"You got some fucked up see through skin," one boy said. "You black or you blue? What the fuck is you?"

I looked up at the kid before I responded. Must be in 6th grade—one of the kings of this elementary. And here I was, just another first day—a bunch of first days.

You got some momma to teach you to talk like that. What is you? I thought to say. But I didn't say it out loud. I only said it in my brain, on the inside. Where people could see anyways. Maybe he would see me thinking it.

"I got poison in my blood. My hemo-goblin. If I bleed don't let it touch you or you'll get cyanosis."

I did say that part out loud, and waited for him to get mad. He didn't get mad. He smiled and then he laughed.

"You is a freak," said the middle boy with hair shaved so close you could see where his skull and jawbone connected when he talked.

He looked sideways at his two friends, one who let his uniform shirt hang out announcing he was on somebody's side but it wasn't the teachers, the other with a tooth missing making it impossible for him to try and act older than 11. They were smiling, all three of them, looking down on me like a three-headed monster.

"Right, you a freak," one of them said again.

If I smiled along with them it would make it okay for them to call me names forever. That I thought it was funny he called me a freak. And I couldn't smile because my stomach hurt, my chest burned, my heart beat faster and the oxygen in my blood was too thin. Daddy slept in this morning, like he forgot it was the first day of school, so I was late and missed my meds. I would take them right away when I got home.

"I'm a new 6th grader so get used to it," I said. I gave eye contact with each of them, one at a time, from left to right, waiting for a comeback. Their silence meant maybe I had some power. They didn't move and seemed ready to leave. I would be alone again.

"But you want to see something for real?" I asked.

"What you got?"

"You can see my veins."

I pulled up my shirt a bit to show my skinny belly. The faint lines of blue veins criss-crossed under my skin like a highway map. My hipbones at the edge of my pants turned my sad looking belly button into a mixing bowl.

One of the boy's fingertips touched my tummy. I flinched, but it really didn't feel so bad.

"My legs when I'm cold show the biggest blue vein. And," I said, and paused, making them wait for the rest, "you can even see my heart, my beating defective heart, but I ain't gonna show you that."

"I want to see your beating heart."

"No."

"Come on! Can you really see it? What does it look like?"

I pressed my forearm down against my shirt. His arm was at the bottom, lifting it up, not real hard, but he wasn't going to stop. Even though he was a boy, I felt like I was stronger than him, only there were three of them in front of me. *You can't really see it, I was lying, I made that part up,* I wanted to tell them. All they might see was a gross looking scar where they cut me. If they could really see my heart, they would see it pumping out fire right now.

All of this was wrong.

I finally kicked my foot up really hard, right between his legs. My foot made contact, I felt something squish, and he gasped for air, bent over, and covered up with his arms. His friends were shocked silent. I had shattered something that wasn't supposed to break.

What was next? My heart pounded, my lungs burned, and my skin felt frozen but my blood felt hot. I got ready to spring to my feet and run away when someone from the school stepped in.

"What is going on here? Get up young lady. Get up and come here."

It was the lunch lady. Someone I had never seen, but she had that lunch person stance. Her sad, old face was stuck in a permanent grimace.

Next thing I knew, the lunch lady had a hold of my hand and was pulling me inside the school. She led me through the hallways and my vision got hazy. Her grip was too tight, and kids were stopping and staring and making faces. I didn't even know what I was in trouble for.

"Sit here," the woman said and pointed, and she slipped into the school counselor's office.

I sat still and looked down at my shoes. They were so grey. I tapped my big toes together and heard the plastic go tap-tap. Two secretaries eyed me from behind their desks so I looked up and smiled back. If I smiled just right, they would be nice to me. If I looked sweet enough, they would be like kind mothers. I didn't want them to know I was here because I was in trouble. I didn't want them to know I was all sick inside, even though I felt dizzy and ready to faint.

The lunch lady slipped out of the counselor's office and held the door without saying a word. I walked in just as silent. The counselor was a woman with blond hair and makeup on and long eyelashes. Her fingernails had designs. Her nose was big and pointy but the rest was pretty. I wanted her to smile but she didn't, but she wasn't mad either. I couldn't tell if the temperature in the room was hot or cold but something didn't feel right.

The counselor said a bunch of things, but it wasn't until she said, "Ms. George was just worried about you is all," that I thought maybe this was no big deal.

I finally had the chance to tell her what happened. That I was just showing some boys my skin and I got scared. That they didn't hurt me, and that I was sorry. It seemed like I said enough to be allowed to go. But it wasn't.

"Am I in trouble?"

"No, you are not in trouble. We are worried about you. Ms. George thought she saw bruises, or that you weren't eating. Or both. Are either of this true?" the woman asked this but then her cell phone buzzed and she looked away. She put up one finger in the air as if to say *wait, one second*.

I had one second to figure out how to respond.

I knew I wasn't supposed to say certain things. I was not supposed to say that when the heat shuts off we use the stove to keep the house warm until my doctor writes a note to the electric company that I will die if they don't turn the power back on. I wasn't supposed to say that I stay alone sometimes when I get home from school and that my dad gets mad and fights but he doesn't hit me, he just hits walls. I would not talk about my dad and the friends he has over, or that I drink my Grandma's chocolate Ensure shakes if I get hungry and there's no food. I wouldn't even admit to my friends that the first of the month is my favorite because that's when the new food stamp money comes.

I moved my eyes about the room looking for help. There were posters on the wall with sayings and pictures trying to convince kids not to be bad. On the counselor's desk was a picture of her in a white wedding dress. A man was kneeling down in front of her, about to slip a ring on her finger. I knew they were just acting, but both of them were smiling and seemed so happy. This woman would be a mommy soon. Maybe then she'd leave and not care about kids at this school. Or maybe she was the stick-around type, even if the man in the picture stopped being happy and left.

The counselor's voice shifted in tone and the phone call ended with a plan for "training the staff on autism" and "putting it on the agenda" and now her attention was back on me.

"I don't have bruises, I have a heart problem," I said as soon as I saw the counselor's eyes.

"You have some medical problems?"

"Sigh-o-netic Heart Defect" I said. When I said it wrong like this in front of doctors, they would correct me, but here it wouldn't matter. The counselor was no doctor and wouldn't know the difference, but would feel sad for me right away.

"But there is food in your house, right now, if I came over?"

"Women like you don't come on my street."

"Why not?"

"They just don't. Don't make me say. They don't."

"Well, I do."

I realized I hadn't answered the question about food yet. I would answer if she pushed and say, *Yes, there was some.* I wanted to practice not answering things to people. If you answered things right away, they expect you to always answer.

The phone rang again and the counselor answered and held up one finger in the air same way as before. "No, he's suspended. Maybe expelled. No, we can't have an IED because he is not coming back. Yes, they are pressing charges. Yes, they did have to do surgery. They won't try him as an adult but he's at home. Protective service will find a place. Alternative school. I can't help you out here. Not again. Not now."

The counselor hung up fast on this one.

"Lilly, what I mean to say is—we're concerned. What do you eat? Did you eat today?"

"Yes. I had breakfast and lunch but I didn't eat much because I was nervous. I forgot to take my medicine."

I said too much and my heart knew it. My breath picked up, and each exhale had particles of my bubbly stomach inside. My mouth watered with a burning liquid.

"Your parents do make sure they give you your medicine I hope?"

I wanted to say yes, but that wasn't always true. Last time when I couldn't breathe and my heart fluttered, I went to the hospital for two nights. The social worker had talked to my dad about medicine refills. He lied, and I think she knew it, so she set us up with mail order refills. Now I take the Digoxin pills that come in the mail. Dad hardly sees them, but I don't mind, because this way he can worry about Grandma's pills. All three of us take pills that fill up our cabinets.

The counselor waited. I didn't say a word.

I wanted to go home. I wanted to be on my couch with my nose smushed against the cushion, smelling cigarettes and my Grandma's breathing treatment and maybe even Dad with a sack full of White Castles. I didn't answer the counselor but looked at a big poster on the wall about bullying, and pretended to be real interested. I read it to myself and mouthed the words. *Don't be a bystander. Say something. Stopping Bullies starts with you.*

"I will be lunching with you tomorrow, and all next week," the counselor said, finally rescuing me. "Come to my office at lunchtime. Okay? You and me. Now go, shoo... and I do go down your street, or we send someone. That's what we do, when we have to."

She gave me the motion with her hand to leave and picked up her phone. I got up with a smile that I hoped she saw and moved to the door.

My stomach cooled, my blood thickened, and I breathed easy the rest of the day. My teacher, Mr. Edwards, gave me a green folder and a calendar for my mom to sign each day to prove she saw my assignments. He didn't know I don't have a mom, but my dad can sign it just the same.

I sat on the plastic seats of the bus by myself the ride home. Boys threw things, girls got their hair picked at, but I was lucky enough to be left alone. Everyone was excited about school and the promises for the year. Maybe it had some promise for me, too. Mr. Edwards was a man teacher and he seemed good enough for a full school year and made everyone feel safe. If any of the boys on the bus got close to me, I was ready to kick them again.

Ciara and Ciana's mom was there at the bus stop to pick them up like always. She was nice and said hi to me with the same happy face she had for her own kids. The two girls held their mom's hand and I walked next to them. I liked when they were nearby. It was like we were sisters.

We walked by their house and I wanted their mom ask me to come over. It happened last year once in a while. It didn't today. I had a dad, and they didn't, so I guess it's fair that we're all missing something. I tried my best not to say anything about their step-daddy who was in jail, because I knew that would be mean. I was real mean to them once. They told me my house smelled because my Grandma is a witch. I got so mad and said, "Grandma is a witch, and she will dig up your dead dog and put it in a pot to boil and make a potion to kill both of you."

I hated myself for saying that, and wanted to put it back in my mouth, but it was too late. Now Ciara looks at me like she's scared.

They walked up the driveway of their house and I was alone for six more houses. I looked down at the uneven sidewalk blocks thinking to myself, *step on a crack, break your momma's back, step on a crack, break your momma's back.*

I walked to this beat with a jump to my step, like my legs were a couple of drumsticks banging on the earth. My backpack bounced to a rhythm against my back. My empty belly sizzled. The bare lining was being digested by stomach acid, but there were just a few houses to go, and being in my own house would make me feel better inside.

But first a look at the burned down house.

I could have crossed the street before I got there, but I always felt like I had to look inside. The house was like me. Burnt up a bit with enough holes that you could see its insides.

The walls were all charred like a piece of chicken that fell into the barbeque pit. Walls were crumbled, there were holes in the roof, and the windows were broken so that they looked like eyes and a mouth, always watching me. The people came to board it up once or twice, but somebody always graffitis the boards first, and then later rips them down. Inside people do drugs in the darkness. *The "man" was going to demolish it some day*, is what my dad said, but the *man* never came.

Dad once told me my mom used to live there, but he was drunk that day. He said that Mom then went away because she was sick in her belly but then she died. I didn't believe most of what he told me. Dad couldn't look at me when he tried to make this stuff up and would make excuses to leave. I would ask the same exact question about mom getting sick, and Dad would change his story many times. "Her belly was hurt" or "the doctor's messed up the operation," or "she choked and couldn't breathe." His answer would switch and he'd always look at his left shoe and move it around like he had gum on it.

He will never tell me what really happened. I knew my mom didn't really live there, but if she did, I wanted to be nearby.

There was somebody who had been living there off and on for as long as I remembered—a homeless man who seemed like a ghost haunting the place. He would go away for a long time, but always came back—sometimes days later, sometimes months.

But he was there now. I peered into the ruins and saw his shadow in the door. He was not sleeping this time, but pacing back and forth. His back was partly hunched and his arms swayed with each step. He seemed full of energy, like he was feeding off the discarded trash of the street. A shroud of dirt surrounded him and I tried to peer through the haze. He saw me looking and started pacing my way. Was he coming to me or would he turn back around? His eyes were on mine, his steps brought him closer, and I needed to do or say something

My legs were stuck. I felt my heart valve misfire and leak just like the doctors said happens. He stood before me. My eyes went big. He knows who I am. It's like he recognizes me or just likes me because we both have weird skin. His skin was a strange shade and changed colors in different places, and his face was gruff. His eyes were like my dad's eyes, tough eyes that men get from living on this street. His arms kept patting his pockets. I needed to do or say something.

"Good day, mister."

He mumbled something back, looked up, turned, and paced back to the house. His boots went bang bang bang back up the porch.

I moved on across the street to my home.

*FROM THE AUTHOR – *Severely mentally ill homeless men living in abandoned houses is pretty common to Detroit or any major city.

My time around such schizophrenics who have audio and visual hallucinations has always been amazing. Most schizophrenics are uniquely intelligent but are simply not built for this world. Some would say that they don't see things that aren't there, they actually see and hear everything that is there. Stimuli that you and I miss they pick up, and all of it makes them incapable of living. They hear the tiny thoughts inside all of us that most learn to ignore. They hear the wavelengths that aren't in our range, and see color schemes that we dismiss.

They live in the corners of our world and in places like abandoned houses. Here is more from the gentleman who is inside of me and begging to be let out.

Chapter Five: Jervis the Squatter

That girl was real. She wore a backpack that he heard bouncing on her shoulders. She had skinny legs. She had white dotty eyes. Her skin looked veiny and blue, like something he might have made up from his thoughts. But he knew it wasn't a hallucination. He wasn't dreaming. He felt the heat of her eyes looking at him.

"Good day, mister," she had said.

He rubbed a palm over his chin and felt the bristle of beard growth. The scratches made a loud noise to his ears, and he wondered if others could hear the sound. It helped him think to rub his palm over his beard hair. He put a pinky in one of his ears and twisted to scratch. Then he pulled up his yellow pants by the belt loops and paced.

Pacing back and forth stopped his thoughts from swirling away from him. He had to walk with them to keep them from spilling over. He had to move fast enough so they didn't whirl. He controlled his brain that way, walking with enough speed to keep his roller coaster mind from doing corkscrews.

Did he have everything?

Time to check again. He patted his front pocket and felt the food stamp card. Check. He patted the other pocket for his state id. Check.

He was safe. Living was good.

Today there would be no snow, not even close. He knew his account number to withdraw money. 3547. He had 20 dollars left but would save it and eat at the Rescue Mission soup kitchen each day. As long as Kendall don't come by with his group. Or the police. Or some white punk-ass kids trying to pound him again. And as long as it doesn't snow. It won't snow. It's hot enough to make him sweat, but he liked that. And soon he would have his social security disability money on the first of the month. How long did he have? Twelve days until the direct deposit. Friends would come by then, but for now he would walk.

And Jervis walked.

Then he did a safety check again. Patted one pocket then the other. Weather check, 3547 remembered. And twelve days left to wait, or maybe two days? But he had 20 dollars still.

The girl was real. He figured that out already. He watched her walk down the sidewalk more than once and onto her porch across the street. The house swallowed her and she disappeared. But she was real. The boy that sometimes walks around this place, he was not real.

Damn he needed to shoot some dope to stop his brain completely for a while. Addicts are always walking this street. Weak, rail skinny addicts with dope in their blood. He could nab one of them.

Milk-Blood. *Not again. No. Don't.*

Maybe he needed a fifth of five-o-clock vodka, or a couple 40 ouncers. Something to keep his head straight. Pacing was tiring, mumbling wasn't fun.

He had his first hallucination at six years old when he saw a mouse. Like a flash out of the corner of his eyes the brown critter scurried from behind the toaster, over the stove top, and then dashed behind the cabinet. It was not a big rat, but one of those tiny mice that were often behind couches and chairs in his house. He went after it, looked in the cracks between the cabinets, but couldn't see it anywhere. Where did it go? It couldn't have gone far. Even though they were speedy, he'd caught some before, (and when he did, had no idea what to do with them).

The strange thing about this mouse was that it made no noise. All of the other mice made crazy fast *pitter-patter* noises when they ran. Sometimes at night he would hear them outside his bedroom door scurrying across the kitchen.

It's only real if you see it *and* hear it, he concluded. Otherwise, it's just your own thoughts lying to you. That's what helps him get by when he hears the voices telling him he's *bad*, and that he should *cut himself* and *kill himself.* If you can't see what's talking, it's just your own thoughts lying to you.

This realization came after many suicide attempts, the first being one in high school with an X-Acto knife from art class he hoped would satisfy the voices inside. He loved that knife, and wished they hadn't taken it away. It cut better than anything and didn't hurt. The blood from that knife brought the best blood of all.

Soon, mental health teams came to his house for *therapy.* They said things like, "Jervis has an illness, it's not his fault. It's a family disease."

"His dad's in prison. He's a monster and a junkie," his mom would answer.

The *therapy* went into his brain and he waited and listened until they left. Medication bottles followed with pills that turned everything off and made him eat too much and bloat up like a fat pumpkin. He became gross, got angry at girls, then he'd stop taking the medications and try to carve himself up.

He went to a home for kids where they would do five-point take downs when the voices inside won and made him escalate. They dragged him to the "quiet rooms" where he was locked inside and made noise with such energy for hours. When he left the home for good, they gave him a paper GED and everyone clapped. More medications followed.

Then Dad died in prison, and the ashes were delivered to his mother's house. Jervis went home too, and lived in the basement along with the ashes. Just like his father he fell in love with smack. Heroin. For Jervis, it was the best medication to stop the voices in his head. Heroin, weed, liquor, all of it armed him for the fight.

He had a pretty good run living in his mom's basement, until he fucked up. He stole—too much. He was so full of drugs he had to. Then his mom stopped that, and the thing happened with his dad.

That thing in the basement.

Milk-Blood.

3547 is all I need to keep money so I don't have to do it again.

After the basement thing happened his violence exploded. Jails followed in different counties. Wayne, Oakland. Macomb. Oakland again. He got haircuts before seeing judges, had psychiatric evaluations, and lawyers told him to "stand mute" before any judge he saw. Incarcerations went from jails to a prison, lithium made the time go by and stopped him from constantly having to be restrained and taken to isolation. If only they would give him a prescription for smack like they do Lithium. As it was, even out of jail, he could only get the drugs after check day. Or he'd have to whack someone outside the house and drag them inside and take their Milk-Blood.

Finding this house kept him out of jail for 12 years. It was the perfect street. The home he always needed. The first time he came here, he had just traded the Oxycontin his Medicaid paid for to get a bottle of Vodka and was looking for a safe place to squat. The house was freshly burnt, abandoned, and quiet with an overgrown lawn. It was asking him to come inside. There was a board on the front door to pull back, but after that, the house was empty and warm.

He slept one night in mostly silence, slept two, and then brought some supplies—an old rug to sleep on, a can opener, and a sack of white socks. He'd have to share his space for a moment or two with white folk coming in to smoke rocks. That wasn't so bad, because if he wanted something they had he'd hit them with a pipe or act crazy enough to scare the shit out of them. People are scared of dirty black men.

Sometimes people were really nice to him. They'd stop by and say things like, "Good day, sir."

The spirits of those who lived in this house before him were still there. He could feel the heat from their body or the whoosh of the air when they walked by. There was a child who died there, who sometimes made voices, and Jervis could feel his memories living inside the walls. How the glass window had shattered and flames filled the front room. The air was so thick that the boy's lungs had filled with black and then he died.

For many days Jervis didn't bother talking to this boy. It was like looking for the rat that was never really there. He just blocked it out. But this rat kept coming back and *pitter-pattering* on the floor.

"What's your name little man?" Jervis asked softly with his lips but loudly with his mind.

"Oscar, I'm Oscar, but they calls me Oz."

"Oz, that's great, Oz. Are you for me or against me?"

"I'm with you is all. With you here. We're stuck."

Every day when the sun started to dip he would hear the shriek of the school bus bringing home the children of the street. The boy would run out to the sidewalk to play with them on their way home, but nobody even knew he was there.

I know what you feel like, Jervis thought. I was like you.

Once somebody dropped a school book and Jervis brought it back to the house for Oscar to read. *James and the Giant Peach*, it was called, and Jervis tried to read it out loud, but there were too many words he couldn't make out. Inside the book, there were exactly twelve pictures that he could look at.

But Oscar loved the book, and finished it fast, and wanted other books to read. All Jervis could do was tell him stories of his own life while the boy sat and listened. They had all the time they needed, and Jervis was good to him like a father might be, but the boy wasn't real. Jervis wanted a real child to make his own.

When bad weather hit and Jervis had no money, he would have to stay sober for a few days, and this made his brain spin faster. The outside crept in, and the world reminded him who he really was. Hordes of voices shot at him from everywhere. Radio waves from other counties. Currents from electrical lines, with birds on the wire standing watch. It was like walking into a spider web you couldn't see and it's too tiny and sticky to get free. The spirits learned how to trap him when he was caught unawares. They would make him do things. Oh, it hurt his head to think about it.

His skin turned red from rage boiling out. His blood burned until his veins were just filled with the ashes of his dad. Being alone and angry was terrible—he needed someone to hurt.

"This is my fucking house…leave me alone," he howled at the boy.

As soon as he said it he wanted to cry. He felt the spirit of Oscar receding. Not leaving but going back into the nooks and crannies that only he could fit inside—back into the insides of this house, back into the rubble in the yard.

Oscar would never be the real child that Jervis wanted, but still, they both belonged in this burnt up house. His lungs were coated with the dust of this place and that would never change. Even though the furniture inside was just piles of ashes, he had a home.

It was good living until the voices became too much and his blood surged with anger. He wanted to hurt people, real people, to inject his hurt into them and make them his own. And eventually, he did hurt people—he did inject people, too many to count. And when he did, his skin wasn't just black, but a raging red fire.

Like the woman from many years ago—it was the spirits that made him do it. They caused his rage and made him grab her and inject her with his deepest parts. She ran off with parts of him inside of her and left behind a puddle of milk.

But then she returned. The body of his lover came back. He knew it was her before she came, same way he could see through time to the future or hear brain waves if he just listened right. She arrived in pieces and someone buried her under the land.

Dead. Now she was dead. Jervis could hear her cry through the earth. It kept him up nights. He squeezed his own temples hoping it would stop, but it just got worse and felt like a dentist drilling into the side of his skull. Finally he went to the spot she was buried. He lay there and pressed his face to the ground.

"Why are you so sad?"

"I'm dead. He killed me."

"You're dead but you're not done yet."

"I know."

"Why don't you come up?"

"I can't, he burned me and cut me up and buried me."

"I can help you," Jervis said. "You can come into me. Spirits done that in the past."

"No, I don't want help from the likes of you," she answered. "There is another. I have gone into his head. I can do that. I can get in people's skulls."

"Whose head? Who is he?"

"Someone who will help. I will see to it."

"You don't need him. I can get you your daughter. I'm the one."

"You are rotten. I feel the rotten parts of you."

"But I can help."

"You will bring my daughter to me?" she asked.

"Yes. I see her often."

"What did you put inside me that day?"

"It was supposed to feel good, but bad things…I do them sometimes," he said. "I didn't kill you."

"You ripped me apart and put something inside of me," she cried.

"But now you have a daughter."

"That girl is your girl too. You fathered her."

"Mine?"

"Yes, your girl too. Bring her to me," she whispered.

So Jervis paced, back and forth, and the roller coaster in his head got faster with higher climbs, longer falls, and many twists. He checked his pocket, felt the slight outline of his food stamp card and his ID. Recited 3547 to himself. *She is my girl too?*

Still, the woman cried, all night and much of the day, like a baby who was sick. It made Jervis dream about sharp knives and sirens and ice storms. His head was glass and ready to shatter. This had to end.

"I. Will. Get. Her. For. You." Jervis said, mumbling one word with each step. Then he turned around and repeated himself, "I. Will Get. Her For You." Turned. "I. Will get. Her for you." Turned. "I will get her for you."

Six words and six steps and it was soothing at first, but then maddening. Energy flowed harder, his words gained power.

"IwillGetHerforYou."

And he turned.

"IwillGetHerForYou."

And he turned.

"IwillGetHerForYou."

It rocked his insides, became a drumbeat, faster and louder. Red rage poked like goose bumps through his skin.

He watched the girl across the street step onto her front porch and then inside the door. His girl. A small girl who got eaten up by houses. Getting her would be easy.

Chapter Six: Lilly Home From School

I bounced onto my porch to the smell of cigarettes and ashes. They were fresh, I could tell, because the ashes kind of stayed in the air the way they do—like tiny bits of them were still floating.

No cars were in the driveway, so I checked the front door with a little prayer in my head and a twist of my hand and it spun. It was open. *Whew...* that was nice.

The room was dark. No noise. But there was something inside that seemed different. Like I was in the wrong house. Or maybe I was the wrong person.

I opened the door all the way and saw why. Uncle Nelson was there, sitting in my daddy's chair in front of the TV. Next to him his new baby boy Joey was sleeping. Where was the boy's mom?

I kept a hand on the doorknob, ready to leave like my dad asked me to if Nelson was acting too weird. Or being too drunk. Or smoking stuff. That was the worst. He didn't smell like that now though. He smoked things other than cigarettes sometimes and I know what that smelled like.

"Hey kid, just waiting on your dad. Right?"

I nodded and looked away. I didn't want to see Nelson right now so I wouldn't look at his eyes. I refused to, but felt his eyes on me, trying to make me look. I looked down at the baby seat. They carried Joey in that thing everywhere, and then just slipped it in their car. I could hear their car a mile down the road. I thought about lifting the baby out of the seat but didn't want to be anywhere near his daddy, Nelson.

"Okay," I said, giving Uncle Nelson an answer to make him happy, and went to the kitchen to get some bread. There was half a loaf that had started to mold, but I flipped deep down into the thin bag and found one that was the best. I toasted the bread because I heard that makes it less stale and kills the bad stuff. The peanut butter melted onto the hot bread and spread easy with the knife. The first bite burnt my tongue but tasted so good and creamy.

Cigarette smoke drifted in from the other room. I licked the peanut butter off the knife and my tongue rubbed a bit on the sharp side, but the knife was too dull to really hurt. My mouth watered and my stomach made acid ready to digest and burn the sandwich up. The bread would soak in the flames.

"Your dad. When's he gonna be in?"

He yelled from the other room and his words hurt my ears. He wasn't going to pretend I wasn't there like I hoped. I didn't want to talk to him. I wanted the TV to myself.

"Well when's he gonna be in? I need to see him."

Dad was probably at the doctors with Grandma, but I wasn't going to tell him anything.

"He doesn't like it when you're here," I said real loud, and then hurried over to see if this made him mad. His face wasn't mad but was silent and staring, making me wait for his response. And he knew I was waiting for his reaction, too. I took another bite of my sandwich, and made the mistake of looking in his eyes.

His eyes were grey, and looking at them turned my skin a colder shade of blue. They swirled like a fingerprint, round and deep into a blackness that sucked me in. I could feel it in my chest. They reminded me what a dead persons eyes must look like. Black flashlight beams.

His body slacked in the chair, and his skin was a strange kind of yellow. He had so many moles on him it was hard to tell what was mole color and what was skin color.

"This time is different. I don't need nothing, I got to talk to him."

Whatever it was, he seemed happy with it. He took a puff of his cigarette and leaned back into my dad's chair.

"Sick of waiting. Too Sick. Too sick." He mumbled to himself but also seemed happy to have an audience.

He stretched out his leg to put a hand in his pocket, and pulled out a vial of his *medicine*. He held it in front of his eyes, like he wanted me to see it too, and thwacked it with a finger. He poured the tiniest bit out on the table while I chewed the last of my sandwich.

I knew what he was going to do. I'd seen him do it once through our cracked bathroom door before. "I'm shaving Lilly," he told me, then shut the door the whole way. He tried to hide it and pretend I couldn't see, but I knew, and I know he goes into our basement for it sometimes too. The spoons, the syringes, a lighter, I seen it before and didn't want to watch it again. But if I didn't sit there and stay with him, I feared something worse was waiting for me, so I remained. Plus, I wanted to watch over Joey in case he woke up.

Nelson looked like an old, dirty nurse as he made up his potion. I waited for any sound of my dad—a car door slamming, the creak of the doorknob, or his voice yelling at me to put my shoes away. But there was nothing. Nobody was coming.

Finally, he held up the needle to his eyeball and I knew he was ready. My nurses always do the same when I get blood taken, right before they tell me it won't hurt too bad. I never believed them. What I really wanted to know is if it hurt them to poke me—if they imagined it when they punctured my skin again and again, or if they forget what it's like. Some can still feel it, I can tell, but most don't remember anymore and stop feeling anything.

"Where's Joey's momma?" I asked. I really wanted to know.

"She'll be here. She had to see her worker. That's why I'm here. Need to ask your dad something. Right...she'll be back."

He was looking at me again. *I should have been quiet.* I felt his eyes on my feet and go up my legs. I smashed my knees and shoes together. My white uniform shirt was untucked, and I slowly crossed my arms over my chest to protect my defective heart beating beneath.

Still he stared while his cigarette smoke was seeping into my lungs. I could taste it. The smoke irritated my insides, like tiny ashes were floating down my throat, and I wanted to cough but held it back. It seemed important I stay still and not flinch. Stay strong.

Grey eyes swirled round and round faster into me, but then he stopped and went back to fixing up his medicine. It was like I had passed a test, for now.

"You don't tell your dad I'm doing this right now, right?"

I shook my head no. I don't tell my dad most things.

"Good. But damn, you still all blue and veiny, right? Wish I had those veins right now."

He started slapping his arms. Smack, smack. Then he tied something around his muscle and his saggy skin got trapped. He flipped the arm over to its underside, made a fist, released, made a fist, released. He held the needle and paused, and it seemed like that moment right before a magician works his magic. The waiting ended, I took a breath, and his eyes bugged out of his head and he stuck the needle in his arm.

I flinched when it hit, like I was the one being poked, and I even felt a rush through my body and expected to feel it hurt. But it didn't hurt him. I watched how he pulled out some blood, then pushed in, and heard him exhale. He exhaled so deep I could smell his insides come out. Something seemed to lift right out of him, like a ghost coming up out of his body, rising through the ceiling, and it was gone.

"There…there…there…now. Where's your dad. Oh, man. Sorry little Lil'. I been so uptight. I don't feel right without my medicine. When's your dad gonna take care of you? You seeing doctors?"

"Yes, I might have to get another operation."

He rolled his eyes and his body sunk into the chair. He put the vials back into his pocket.

"What does your medicine do," I asked. The words were sticking in my mouth. I needed something to drink. The peanut butter made me feel all sticky inside.

"It takes away the pain, makes me feel like I'm supposed to. Stops my back from hurting, stops me from wanting to puke. Makes me happy. It takes away the rotten parts of this life that we are living."

His eyes circled the room as he said this, and then they landed right on me.

"You got pain," he said, and then got up and started pacing. He scratched his back, and sniffed snots in his nose.

"We all got pain," he told me. "It's this fuckin life. Cursed life we live, not worth the trouble to have to live it in pain. It's unnatural. You're proof of that. You don't want to live forever like you are, do you? This medicine is just a reminder from the Lord."

"A reminder of what?" I asked, but was afraid to look up and see his eyes, so I looked down. I shuffled my feet, pointed my shoes towards each other and tapped them, tap tap.

"A reminder of what we should feel like instead of how we do in this sick world. Until you have medicine to make you see the beauty and make you warm, life is a sickness I have—a fucking curse. I don't feel well. Ever. But what the fuck do you know? You're a child."

"I feel like that sometimes."

"That's because you've been sick since you been born. You shouldn't be alive some say. You're a miracle. That person you call Dad…well, there's more to that story."

"What more to that story?" I asked, and looked down at Joey sleeping who seemed plenty happy and didn't need any medicine.

"What more?" I asked again. I really wanted to know what Uncle Nelson meant. I could feel him breathing and getting ready to talk. His skin seemed looser on his body, his muscles moved fluid like water, and he was soft where before he was hard. There was even some kindness to his eyes.

"There is no story, really. You don't want to know. You're ten now, right? Ten. That's cool. We can do something else to show you. But just a little. You want some of my medicine? I can tell you want some. Lemme fix you up."

My heart thumped and sent shock waves through the rest of my body. Joey flailed his legs on the ground, and then settled back in without waking.

"Yeah, I did it first at twelve. You can do it now. You're not a regular kid, you know that."

I didn't object, and it seemed liked the decision was made. I watched him sit back down and go through his procedure, like a doctor ready to operate. He turned off the TV like I was supposed to hear something. The silence hurt my ears and made the moments tick.

"Your dad doesn't like me here because I know everything. I know what happened. I knew your momma. Yep, I knew your momma. You tell that person you call daddy that we did this, and you will have more trouble from me and from him. But you know that, right?"

He stopped and stared, and I shook my head yes.

"Now you ready to feel good?"

I shook my head yes again. Of course I was ready to feel good.

"Well this is the best you will feel until you die. This defective heart shit you got, whatever it is, it ain't going away. The doctors are going to cut into you until you die. If I was you, I would go get the person who did all of this. Get back at them. That will take your hurt away as much as this fucking dope."

When he punctured the needle into me, I felt part of my insides escape from me forever, and the empty space was being filed with something new, something thick, and something alive. Right away my body felt so warm. Not on-fire warm, but warm like a blanket just out of the dryer that you put up to your cheek. Everything loosened. Cells that were tight, relaxed and began to float. My uncle became the perfect nurse who understood me more than my doctors did, and filled me with medicine that was from my own home, not the world of hospitals with white walls, but from my street where I woke up to everyday.

"You got it? Good. I'm gonna do a big huge blast o'fucking crack rock. Big fuckin blast o'rock for some homemade speedball. I never shoot this shit, why waste a fucking vein… don't watch this part."

Was he talking to me or not talking to me, I wasn't sure, because I started to feel as sweet as a baby, like Joey lying on the ground. It was Beautiful. But I couldn't call it beautiful because everything was beautiful so how could one thing be called beautiful if everything was the same. The baby knew this, that's why he slept, and now I was being invited into his perfect world.

Nelson told me not to watch him, but I did anyway. He was waving the flame of his lighter over a tiny glass pipe and started sucking so hard to keep everything in until he exploded in a huff. I saw a look on his face like he was taking a poop, everything strained so tight and his grey eyes whirled like crazy while smoke flew out of his mouth. His body was jerky, like random pieces of invisible strings were yanking him from the ceiling. I could feel his nerves twitch, and after he blew out another puff of smoke he started pacing to the windows, peeping out the broken shades, saying, "They been watching us…they're coming. They know what we do."

They aren't watching, they're beautiful too. All of them, I wanted to say. I didn't care he was paranoid. I wasn't leaving here ever.

With his second puff of smoke my dream started. I was Joey's twin, his better part, and could feel each of his breaths in my own chest. I was a baby again and healthy as could be. I wasn't defective. Why did I ever believe otherwise? Tiny spots of me bubbled with happiness until the bubbles were everywhere. With one finger I traced the underside of my arm and looked at the tiny puncture wound from the needle. I had found a tiny hole in me to put God inside. God and teachers don't come on my street, but they were inside of me now.

When my dad got home, I was holding the baby. Joey's flesh on mine was the most amazing thing. I had been sitting there feeling his smooth skin and tracing his arms down to his little fingers. The tiny wrinkles in his fingers and the tiny little nails were amazing. I imagined I was Mary and he was Jesus and I just had a baby. That was how good I felt. This must be how regular people feel always, everyday.

My dad barely gave me a glance when he got home but set Grandma in her spot and talked to Nelson in the other room.

When I lay in bed that night, with the door cracked, I could hear Dad and Nelson with some friends. I didn't care when I smelled the metallic smoke coming from the living room and the sound of men in the hallway. Nothing scared me now.

When the morning came, I wasn't sure if I had slept all night or just dreamed, but the good feelings had left me. Burning bile started to eat away at my warm spot, my stomach ached with need for food, and my spine hurt the worst.

I was going to need more medicine.

Chapter Seven: Lilly Back at School

It was recess. My belly had a bowl of cheerios and a Pop-Tart in it so far. It was a frosted Pop-Tart. Plus I had half a banana, but not the whole thing since it had brown spots and those parts made me sick.

Yesterday, I had lunch with the counselor lady who asked me all sorts of questions. She said the world wasn't a fair place but that I probably knew that, but when it tips far enough out of balance that someone should come and help. She had a license that made her contact people who would visit my house—from the state. They watched over things. I listened, but knew not to say too much. I didn't speak on things like what's in the fridge and the roaches under the fridge and my dad's friends who come over sometimes. I definitely wasn't going to tell them about the medicine that Uncle Nelson gave me.

And I know it's not medicine. It's heroin. Or H. Or dope. Or smack. But I like to say medicine.

Lunch with the counselor for one day was all it was, not all week like she promised, so at recess I went back to my place sitting with my back to the wall. Sitting there twice was enough to claim it as mine.

The same three boys came to me again. One still had his shirt untucked, like he had to fix it each day to make it that way. The others were tucked in like the school policy said it had to be, but I saw on their faces something different, something schools don't reach or get to control, like that space behind your fridge. They saw it in me too.

"Are you going to show us your heart or not?"

"It's fixed."

"How did it get fixed?"

"They injected me right here, and now it's fixed."

I showed them the tiny little mark like a chicken pock on my underarm. I knew my heart wasn't really fixed, but it just felt like that. If I could feel like a normal person for just a bit, then maybe I belonged. I wasn't so strange, wasn't so different from the boys next to me. The boy traced the big blue vein of mine up and down my underarm with his finger. It felt good.

"But they still have to cut me open again."

They left me alone, and didn't want to see my heart anymore. The day dragged on just the same.

Later on, two girls got into a fight, and lots of boys laughed and screamed to root them on. The teacher had to leave us alone, and our classroom was empty when the bell rang. We didn't get our homework assigned before the day ended, and I smiled right away thinking about home and the day before. Maybe I'd get some medicine again.

I felt older all of sudden, but also like I was just born.

The school bus bounced over holes in the street and shook my insides. When they got to my stop and the door opened, cool air got sucked into the bus and brushed against my skin. Colder days were coming.

I walked with Ciara and Ciana and their mom, but didn't want to be invited to their house. My legs moved fast down the sidewalk, brushing past the cracks but never stepping on them. Nothing could stop me. Home was different now. And Joey needed me.

I could feel Ciara's mom watching me down the sidewalk, like she does sometimes to make sure I'm safe.

I walked by the abandoned house and looked to see if it was any different after everything that had happened. It stood there rotting just the same. The man was inside, moving fast again, and pacing back and forth, more like a robot than a person. I saw him through the front doorway, and he'd walk and disappear, walk and disappear.

But then he saw me and stopped and both of us looked at each other.

I felt a small whoosh, like something had just passed me by, but I was alone on the sidewalk. My legs wanted to move, my chest wanted to stop, and my insides were torn. I thought about waving. But a soft male voice inside told me, *Stop, there's nothing here for you today*, so I dashed across the street. The man watched, I could tell he was watching, but I was safe back home.

I twisted the door knob, twice, both ways. It wouldn't budge and was locked. I tried again with my weight moving left to right and right to left. Nothing. Maybe Dad was with Grandma at the doctors again. Or maybe she was asleep upstairs and he was gone. I could climb up the chimney and get on the roof and see if the upstairs window was open.

Next door, Uncle Nelson's porch was empty. His dark blue Ford Escort with the rust spot that looked like a scab was parked in front. The car was there, so Joey and Nelson should be home. My dad said I could go there if I had to so I did. I left my backpack on the porch and hoped nobody would take it.

Unlike my house, their front door was cracked open. Knocking didn't feel right, so I walked in slowly. The smoke of the warmer air surrounded me. I didn't smell food. I smelled a fight coming.

"Nelson, damn it, get your shit off the washer. I got to use it."

It was Auntie's voice from downstairs. My eyes winced a bit at her screaming, but Nelson didn't move from his spot on the chair. He saw me and smiled. Proud he wasn't moving. Happy to see me back.

"Fuck it, Nelson, your shit's going on the ground," Auntie screamed.

I wanted to go downstairs myself and get the stuff off the dryer and help them both out, but instead I waited to see how he felt about me being here. He made a motion with his head for me to come in. The clothes he had on were the same as yesterday. His t-shirt barely hung over his arms and his pants needed a tighter belt.

Joey was lying on a blanket with a mobile over his head. He had a bottle in his mouth but wasn't drinking it, just clenching the plastic nipple between his teeth so that the bottle hung down his chin. I pushed some of the plastic pieces of the mobile around to make them spin. His eyes went from me, to the red fish floating above him, back to me again. When they spun real fast he'd smile and move his hands and legs like a roly-poly bug on his back.

"You got bleach on my blouse," Auntie yelled from the basement.

Nelson still didn't move. I wanted him to do something. I needed to know if he had his medicine lately or not. A lighter and spoon was right next to him, I saw that right away, and he looked at me different than yesterday. His eyes didn't scare me as much at his house than mine, like he didn't need to scare me anymore. He smelled of smoke of all kinds, not just cigarettes but like a plastic pen was on fire. His bare feet stuck out of his pants, and one foot was swollen and purple. I wished he'd put socks on.

"Come here," he whispered.

I walked over, tiptoed really, ready to take part in this secret deal.

"Hold out your arm. I know that's what you want."

I didn't want to say yes but my whole body was saying yes and there was nothing that could stop it. The memory of the pinprick from yesterday hadn't left me all day. It made my skin think—like it had a mind and voice of its own and was saying *YES*. My heart thumped. Blood sizzled and shot through me. I laid out my arm and turned it to the underside. I was at his mercy. My veins stuck out through my blue-hued skin. I clenched my fist back and forth and moved my fingers like I saw him do yesterday. He made up his batch.

I wanted him to hurry. I wanted my aunt to scream again from the basement again so I'd know she was still down there. If she walked up stairs he would have to stop. This would be over, and I'd be in trouble.

I could hear Nelson breathe through his nose like he was snoring. It reminded me of the noise a sleeping dog makes. No sounds of footsteps from the basement. This was going to happen. He flicked the needle. Pointed towards my arm.

"You got the sweetest blue veins my sweet."

The prick of my skin, and blood was mixing inside the syringe.

A rush went straight from the needle into my spine. An ocean of warm spread from my back and washed over the defects and emptiness inside of me. No longer sick. No longer hungry. Like a hug from a mom—that's what this was. This feeling was something I had been waiting for since the day I was born—the magic to make me feel better. Life wasn't always fair, but now it was.

Nelson looked at my eyes with a knowing smile. I smiled back and lay on the carpet next to Joey. I pushed the mobile and watched the sea of plastic fish swim above me. I picked him up and his skin felt warm against mine. I looked at his face full of dark black skin and pretended that I had the same color skin on me. Like I was his mother. He slept in my arms.

Days went on like this. The weather got colder. School days felt sicker. Boys came by and talked to me. I know they were just teasing me, or pretending to tease me because they wouldn't admit to really liking me. But they talked to me more than before. I was normal. I held back my defective heart beats all day long. Held on while it pumped defective blood all day, until I could go home.

Even if my door was open after school, I dropped off my backpack, and I went next door to Nelsons. My auntie was there, and still they fought. That was okay, giving me the H was somehow part of Nelson's fight against her. I took his side with silent shakes of my head or laughing at him when he mimicked the way she talked. I saw his feet turn darker shades of purple and swell up. I got used to his grey, swirling eyes—as long as he could put the Medicine in me.

Then the day came that changed. I walked home from school and the blue Escort was gone from its usual spot. I hoped that it was just stolen or that they drove together to the store for cigarettes and would be right back. When I checked, and nobody was there at the house, I knew something was wrong.

I sat on the porch. Cars drove by full of boys who I know sold drugs. Girls were with them. Still I waited. Each sound of an engine I thought was the blue Escort. Each minute became the minute before they got there. This was all wrong. Even if they did get home, I may not get anything. Things started to ache inside of me. I looked at my arms, which were just tiny bones with veins in between. They needed to be fed.

I waited. Shadows crept on the house across the street. My dad's car pulled up before Uncle Nelson's did.

"I'm waiting for Joey," I said to my Dad before he could even ask.

"Don't go anywhere else but there, and come right home."

I said okay. He went inside. A long time passed. Cars that came down the street had their headlights on. The grey clouds in the sky turned into a blanket of dark all around. Finally, a pair of headlights pulled in front of Nelsons. Auntie was driving. Joey was in a car seat in the back. No Nelson.

Auntie walked up the driveway carrying the baby seat.

"You here again child? We were at the hospital. They keeping Uncle Nelson. Maybe couple weeks this time. Maybe they have to amputate his leg. Maybe not until they get the drugs out of him. Maybe Methadone. You wouldn't know about all that though. You around to watch Joey? We sure appreciate you coming by here like this. Nelson said he been paying you, but I don't know if he's been lying? How much he paying you?"

The warm hug was gone.

Chapter Eight: Jervis Nabs a Junky

5 days to check day. 3547. The card was still in his pocket. He had ID for food. He paced and listened. He had no choice, the voices were screaming from his insides:

"You're still alive Jervis? You're evil you know that? You're a devil. A red devil. Look at how you rage when you get mad. Cut yourself. Cut yourself right. Be done with it. Cut your own neck. Cut it and watch the blood."

He paced fast and slammed his foot down with each step. The bam bam bam bam of his foot sometimes stopped the voices. Talking to himself blocked them out and turned them into white noise static. But they kept coming, relentless. The voice was mostly his dad, still stuck inside him ever since that day in his momma's basement, but there were other noises too. The little boy Oscar who had nobody to play with. Oscar said he wanted to be like the boy from *James and the Giant Peach* who was saved by magic after his mom and dad were killed. But not him. Not Oscar, he had nothing.

Jervis listened to the boy, but couldn't always hear since the tears of the buried mother made noise all the time. He heard her crying for her daughter. The sound was sharper than any piece of glass he'd ever stepped on. And the little pieces got stuck in his skin just the same.

"When are you going to stop that?" Jervis asked the mother.

"Not until she's with me."

"Why do you think she wants to be with you?"

"I grew her. She gnawed at my insides and clawed her way out. I made her out of nothing and gave her life."

"I put her inside you, she's my girl, she's not all yours."

"You poisoned me."

"I gave her to you."

"The part of her that is sick was from you. You are a fucking red devil."

Jervis would have raised a hand and smacked her when he heard that, but she wasn't there, she was just a noise, not a sight. Just a mouse scurrying on the floor that he could never find. He was done talking with the voices, but they weren't done with him:

"You said you'd bring her to me. Where is she?"

"His dad died, but James got saved by a Giant Peach, who will save me?"

"I will get her myself, get in someone's head and get her."

"Jervis, Jervis. Jeeerrviiiisss"

"You an evil man Jervis. Bad. BAD. A devil. A red devil."

Jervis paced and scanned the street looking for something to help him stop the voices. *Two dogs fighting inside your brain, and you control who wins, the one you feed the most.* That's what they told him once. The mental health team. Well, the voices won't win. He'd pace and talk and mumble them away, or get some dope or get something.

Get my girl.

But his girl from across the street wasn't stopping to see him anymore, so he looked for others.

There was a noise from several houses down that he knew was real. He turned and saw men on the porch. The words were loud, angry. A door slammed, and a man left the house dejected. His head sunk to the ground and he walked defeated. The shroud of smack surrounded him as he approached. Jervis stepped up to greet him on the sidewalk.

"You spare some change?" Jervis asked.

"Fuck off. You think I got change?"

"Well, one can never tell. What you looking for?"

"Nothing. Never mind old man."

"Old man," Jervis mocked, "Well, I may be old but you look same as me. You scrap?"

"Sometimes scrap. Good money, but I got no way to transport it."

"Got some scrap inside."

"Oh yeah. Maybe I got a guy who can come get it. What you telling me for?"

"Can't get the pipes out. Maybe you can help. We can split it."

"Let me see what you mean. Maybe. Maybe."

Jervis saw the look on the man's face. *I can take advantage of him, I can punk this guy*, the man was thinking.

They walked to the house, and Jervis could tell the man had been to prison. He could tell by his walk. By the way he hung his head. By the distant look in his eyes. The man stepped into the house cautious. Waiting for others to be there. His nose crinkled as if the air was about to make him sneeze.

"Bunch of pipes in the basement. Copper. Can't get it down."

They stepped in further and the air of the house engulfed them both. Grey walls were like intestines and they squeezed and squished them in. Thick ashy air was digesting them both, and tiny bits of their flesh were being added to the dead flakes of skin of so many before that coated the floors.

Jervis was home, and the master of this place, and had to do things here even if it made him sad.

The man's head swiveled from side to side, and after pausing enough to make sure he was safe, he walked directly to the basement stairs. Just as he took the first step, Jervis hit the man with the only scrap metal in the house that mattered—a rusted out piece of pipe that fit into Jervis's hand. The man's skull was crushed under the swing of the metal with a squishy thunk, and he collapsed and bounced down the stairs. His bones tangled, twisted, and snapped on one another, and he landed at the bottom like a rag doll. Jervis followed him into the darkness.

There were no lights, and the black air of the place hung thick. It was a tomb. Moans came from the man, deep in his chest. The body still lived. *Good, he isn't dead.* Were his eyes open? Jervis couldn't tell, it was too dark, but one more smash of the pipe and another squishy thunk, and the man was unconscious, moaning no more.

Jervis took out the syringe. It was so dark, he could hardly see it in front of his face, but he could do this blindfolded. He traced his hand and found the man's neck. It was skinny, but warm, and still pulsing with life. There was smack left in this man's veins. There always is. He inserted the syringe into the thick blue vein of his neck. It did get messy, he felt the blood spill, but he pulled back the plunger and captured what he needed and filled his syringe. He took the treasure upstairs.

God it's been a long time since he'd done this. Why no others shared the blood of others this way he didn't know. Probably because it was just him who could do this. He had special powers. Milk-blood. His dad showed him the way years ago.

Jervis pressed the tip of the syringe at his own vein but couldn't get it to plunge. He needed a new needle. This one wasn't sharp. He kept poking until it hit his mark, drew some of his own blood, and then mixed in the new.

Jervis felt a spastic energy, like a quick sneeze or an orgasm. He grunted loud enough to make his chest vibrate. Inside his head, the voices left. New blood pulsed, new thoughts and memories rushed in.

Yes, the man had been to prison. Sexual assault. The man had crack and dope in his blood. Fresh from today. Jervis could feel that as well. The man had kids too, but they didn't talk to him anymore. Jervis could feel the scars that built over the man's hurt that stopped him from caring. The man was as sad as Jervis was, and had traveled the city streets picking up whatever scraps he could find to make life bearable.

And now they were inside Jervis.

3547.
Get my girl.
Stop the voices.
Good living one more day.

Chapter Nine: Lilly Meets Jervis Close Up

I was itching all day at school. My skin felt achy and oozing and tingly. My nose was full of wet, draining snots, and I felt hollow inside even though I ate some. When it came time to write our assignments in our green folder, I wasn't sure if I could make it. I was worried somebody would see me sweat. I wondered who you talked to here if you had to go to the hospital. I knew if they called my dad it would be hard for him to pick me up.

I can make it. I can make it. As long as everybody here leaves me alone.

But they didn't. The counselor called me down to her office and had me talk to another lady who was with her. She wore a badge, had a big brown bag, and asked me all sorts of questions. My answers were short. "Nobody was hurting me," I told her, "I am skinny because I don't eat my dad's dinner," "I have a heart defect so ask my doctor." They were disappointed in me when I left. Whatever they wanted to pull out of me, I didn't want to give it to them. Time to go home.

I had on a blue hoodie with long drawstrings, and underneath my skin was moist with cold sweat. It was not the sweat that drips down your skin, but the kind that bubbles all over you and stays there. My stomach felt like I had to poop, but there was not much in my tummy anyway.

The plastic seats of the bus ride bounced and jiggled my body, and the screechy bus noises vibrated through my temples. I closed my eyes and clenched my whole body together.

"What's up with you?" an older boy asked.

"My heart. I'm getting it cut tomorrow. Don't get close."

They left me alone and I got off at my stop. I avoided eye contact with Ciara and Ciana's mom but she saw me anyways.

"We'll watch you walk home," she said.

I smiled back and looked at the ground and walked fast down the sidewalk as they watched me. It wasn't long until I heard their door slam shut and they weren't looking anymore. The only thing in sight were cars rushing too fast down the street.

Why should I rush? There was no Nelson to go to. He wasn't home. I had to get to something, I just didn't know what.

The smell of the burnt house was in the air. I looked up at the second floor where the window used to be. The big dark opening looked back down on me. If somebody was up there, they'd be able to see everything, but right now, all above was empty and quiet.

I stared at the house the same way I always do, and it helped me forget some of my hurt. It was like a painting where the little details were different each day, and I had to try and guess what had changed. I noticed when the grass changed colors out front, noticed when a new piece of garbage was on the front lawn and when the stray dogs had split the bags open and flung the trash all about. In the spring, I noticed when new trees sprouted from the cracks on the porch. I could always tell if anything different was spray-painted on the sides. The day they boarded it up a year ago (that didn't last) I dreamed it before it even happened.

People try to take care of houses and people with heart defects, but it just doesn't last.

I stood and waited. Usually the man inside was pacing, smoking, mumbling about something, sometimes even other people were with him. But not this time. Nothing moved. Just dead silence.

My gut gurgled like a gross potion was swirling inside, and I felt ready to have diarrhea. I put my hand over my belly as if I could calm it down. Nothing helped. I needed to move, to put something in me, to go somewhere, to call someone. Maybe if I just take Digoxin at home it can help. I can smash it up and eat it the way Dad does with pills to make them work better. Maybe just a peanut butter sandwich will help, but the bread was probably gone. Or tuna. I know there's tuna, but that always tastes gross, and I can never work the can opener right.

Or I could take one of Grandma's Ensure drinks. Dad got mad if I did that, and Grandma always knew when I stole one even if she was asleep and couldn't possibly see me. Every time I'd sneak one, Grandma would smack her lips like a zoo animal super loud. She wouldn't stop until I finished the drink. Made me feel like I was making her starve, and like she was always watching me.

But Uncle Nelson. His stuff would make me happy. He needed to be home soon. Maybe he would come home today. If not I will have to find someone else. I know some boys who know how to get H. I can let them know I am like them, that I can cuss and be as cool as anyone. Maybe I can get an older boyfriend who would hang out with me. I know a bunch of boys… (Darren Marshall, Cory Raymond) but they wouldn't want a skinny-ass freak like me.

Somebody had to help me or I'd go to the hospital and they would put the mask over me so they could cut me open and it would all go away and…

Then I saw something in the grass. It was a foot. A big orange boot. I traced the leg up to his body.

It was the man, the same one as always, lying in the grass. I never been this close to him but there he was lying there right in front of me. His arms were crossed on his chest and his big octopus fingers were locked together. His mouth was slack and open but his eyes were closed. His skin was a strange color, like mine, but older. His hair was scraggly, not long, but like an old man beard. He wasn't moving. Maybe he was dead. Or drunk. I looked up and down the sidewalk—nobody was in sight, and who knows if my dad was even home.

I liked that I could see him and he couldn't see me. Like watching a lion up close at the zoo. His eyelids seemed so flimsy, with barely an eyelash on them. His nose was big and round like a clown's nose. You could tell he didn't bathe. He wore a green army jacket that seemed way too warm, and some dirty purple clothes were under his head.

Then, like a ray of the sunshine peeking from behind the clouds, his eyes opened and he was staring right at me.

He didn't even stir when he woke up like people do, his eyes just flipped open, like he knew I was watching him. I thought to run but something stopped me. *I can handle him. I can do this.*

"Hey Mister."

He didn't say anything back. Next to him was a bottle whose blue label was faded like it had been there for a year. There was a crumpled white McDonald's bag near his head and a drink with the straw sticking out. And tucked at his side, as if he thought nobody could see, there was a syringe. It lay on a twig, sideways, so that together they made a cross.

My feet shuffled ready to move down the sidewalk and cross the street, but my head craned forward to get a better look. *He had a needle.* How good it would feel to get poked right now. Relief. A rush of nice blood would warm my insides. My stomach got mushy just thinking about it.

He didn't move, and the more I stared, the more his faced turned purple-red, like pimples were growing out of his skin. He was an odd monster, like me. He got to his knees, and I took a step backwards, staying out of arm's length.

"Hey Mister," I spoke again.

He pulled himself up to his feet, keeping his eyes on me like he was afraid I would attack him or rob him. I didn't look away but stared right back.

"Your family. They not home," he said

"How do you know?"

"Oh, I just know. I know you."

"You been using the H mister?"

He glanced to his sides and his eyes fixed on the needle.

"Shut up. What do you know about that?"

"I know things. I done H. What the fuck you think I know?"

I have sworn before, but this one tasted different on my tongue and dried it up. I waited for him to react. Instead he said nothing and barely moved. His skin glowed red. His head tilted, like a dog questioning something. It seemed he was listening to a radio station in the other room, some noise that I couldn't hear.

"Needle done make you, needle gonna break you. Now get away before…"

He didn't finish his sentence but swatted his hand in the air like batting a fly.

I took a breath and turned to go home. I had no energy, my bones and muscles ached, and my skin was melting off of me. I was defective. It was too much.

I knew what to do and came up with a plan. The hospital. I hated it there but it was better than being here. I would take too much of my medicine. The whole bottle all at once. I would call the ambulance myself. They would come and bring me to the hospital. Tonight. I can be there soon. Dad won't have to drive me.

The more I thought about it the more I wanted to be there. The white walls and hallways all lit up. Clean blankets. Nurses and medicine. IVs would hurt but the medicine might make me feel better until I could figure this out. And in the morning there would be hot eggs and toast.

It was time to go. I leapt from the sidewalk with two great bounds. My backpack bounced off my shoulders. I was almost to the street and hoped the front door would be open, but if not, I would sneak in through a window on the roof and get inside no matter what.

Then I got tackled from behind.

A huge heavy mass barreled into me, and my little bones smashed to the ground. I knew who it was by the stench. His breath smelled like raw hamburger meat. His skin seemed hot like the outside of a toaster and it glowed red just the same.

His hands clenched so tight that the bone in my arm was getting crunched. His fingers clamped down, and he dragged me across the ground. Each tug pulled at my shoulder socket. I screamed, not in words, but in noises and cries like a car alarm to make others hear. I couldn't kick, my legs were behind me, he was in front. Nobody came so I screamed louder. He dragged my body across the ground and I felt it getting scratched. He had me at the front porch and started to pick me up. I felt so small. The dark mouth of the front door waited.

"Not gonna hurt you my girl," he kept saying. But he already was hurting me.

My dad would come. He had to. Someone would come.

The man scooped me up off the ground and I was engulfed in his arms. My arms and legs were tangled up in a ball. I tried to break free but he had everything bunched up so tight I couldn't do a thing. My hand would start to wiggle and get loose, or my foot moved and tried to kick, and he'd rewrap it back into his grasp.

He was strong. A monster. Nothing like the nearly dead man lying in the grass. And he was crazy. Crazier than any of my dad's friends or Uncle Nelson or anybody. I could feel the crazy.

I heard his boots go *boom boom boom* over the steps of the porch, and he carried me through the doorframe. I turned with one last scream and got a glimpse at my house across the street. Nothing. He was right, my dad wasn't home—just my Grandma somewhere sleeping, and nobody to help.

NOTE FROM THE AUTHOR – I need some dirty, raw, and primitive emotions to write this next chapter. Like tapping into a memory I look inside my shadow self, and let the hurt come forth. Here's what I find:

Chapter Ten: Lilly Trapped Inside

The air inside the house was like a bunch of dust particles that stuck in my lungs. I couldn't get oxygen out of the dirt I was breathing. My heart banged inside my chest. It was ready to explode. It felt like the house wanted me there, like it was hungry and I was its food.

"Stop, stop," I screamed again and again as if he couldn't hear me even though he had me wrapped up in his arms, carrying me into the house. I wanted to say more—to tell him that I was born with a heart defect, to say that you can see my veins because of cyanosis, that I don't have a mommy.

"You think I don't know that?" the man said, like he could hear me think. "You think I don't know? You don't even know who I am. Well you will know, you will see. And you do have a mommy, and she's here. And you even have a daddy."

The man looked down at me. He was carrying me tender and soft in his arms, the way someone would carry a dead body or their newborn baby. But this was all wrong. The house was full of ash and smelled like it was still burning. He carried me through the dark tunnels of the hallway. Shadows of old furniture seemed like people sitting on the ground, watching me, but nobody helping. This couldn't be happening. It was like something had grabbed me and stuffed me into a nightmare.

We went into a room that was the darkest of them all. There were no windows, just a big wooden board where the window used to be, and the tiniest slice of light shooting out its side. A pile of clothes were on a mattress that lay in the corner. He swung his arms forward and dropped me on them. I landed on what felt like a bunch of dirty, moist rags, but I was free.

Do I run? What was happening? He stood before me, legs to his side, waiting to see what I would do. I had to decide. I leapt up to dash away, but with one arm outstretched he held me down.

"Stop it. Just stop it. You here now. You okay. I got something for you. You hungry? You hungry, right? I know this. I'll get you something. You try to leave, I'll put you in the basement. There's others down there. You wouldn't like that."

Others? He left the room and I sat there and imagined the others. I thought about how dark it would be down there. I hated basements. I didn't move.

Plus he was getting me something.

The sound of his boots down the hallway echoed. The room smelled like a fireplace. I curled my legs up into a ball and looked around. Next to the bed were lighters, tin foil scraps, shoes that didn't match each other, and a book. I grabbed the book and tried to read the faint outline of the cover in the dark. Too dark to see.

I stared at the book cover, and a voice came into my head like somebody else was reading it.

James and the Giant Peach

It wasn't my voice, it was a boy's voice. I looked around the room. The walls were dripping with darkness. Stains from smoke were everywhere. I could hear the man's boots. He was back.

"Here you go," he said, and tossed a paper bag that landed next to me on the mattress pile. It was the white McDonalds bag from out front.

"There's a full cheeseburger in there. From last night. Not so bad."

I opened the bag and the McDonalds smell rose to meet me. There was crumbled up napkins and a fry wrapper inside. I reached in and pulled out the cheeseburger. It was smashed like a small saucer, but I unwrapped it, looked up at him, and took a bite. The bun was a bit hard, but the grease made my mouth water.

"Eat you tiny creature. I got more for you."

I finished the first half in two bites. Acid sprayed out from the sides of my mouth, and my stomach felt a burn, but I knew once I swallowed down the cheeseburger, it would soak up the fire inside. I took another bite, and noticed how much I was trembling. Shaking so bad I had to steady my fingers so I could eat. The burger was okay, but I still felt so wrong.

"Now, I know you not okay. Let me look at you though."

He got down on one knee, and it reminded me of the way doctors will look into my eyes and then listen to my heart from the front and the back. His face got close and I could see dirt in the pores of his skin.

"You like the H then little one? You like to shoot it in your skin? Well I got something to inject into your arm. That's what I do."

"I just want to go. When can I go home?"

"Home? You don't think this is home?"

"It's strange here and my daddy is going to kill you." That felt good coming out of my mouth, and I meant it. I waited for him to get angry. I couldn't keep looking at his eyes, so I looked at the door. It was cracked open. There better be a sound from outside soon. Or somebody needed to come. With each breath I took, the linings of my lungs and nose filled up with tiny particles of this place. I would smell burnt up myself by the time I left.

"You think it strange. I know, I know. Strange is you doing dope when you just a tiny thing. But I was like you. People were scared of me, and I was scared of things that weren't there. Heroin turned things off and made me feel so much better. Safe. Strong. Fell in love with it. You and me, we got H for parents we do."

I thought about going for his eyes. Poking his eyes out like my daddy told me to. My fingers wouldn't squish them one bit. My nails weren't long enough but were just chewed up stubs. I could try to kick him. Maybe I would do that in a minute. So far he was just talking. Maybe he would just talk and then let me go.

"What you mean by that?" I said chewing the last bite of the burger.

"You living without your parents. No Mom, no real Dad. You need something."

"I got something. What you got? Why don't you get a job?"

"I got a job. It's master of this house. Master of the whole yard. That's how I met your mother."

He was waiting for me to react to what he said, I could feel it in his breath. My body felt dark, like the room was seeping inside of me. I was drowning in it and had to go.

I felt around for something to grab, like a brick or scissors or a shoe. My hand smoothed over the pile on the bed but there was nothing but the book. I picked it back up, held it on my lap, felt the cardboard spine, and wondered if I could use it to bash the man on the head. Probably wouldn't hurt much, it's just a book. I wished I was in school, at the library, with the teachers yelling at us to be quiet but the boys not listening and the teacher giving up. I would read this book and not goof around and be perfect.

I felt a warmth in my ear, like the breath from someone's whisper, and I heard the boy's voice again. *James had a mom who died too. He lived with some terrible people after that,* he said.

I flipped the book closed and looked down. I decided to obey the man but when my chance came I would dart out of here. There was still no noise from outside. Not a car door slamming. Nothing. Just the sound of another whisper.

James got away in the Peach.

I couldn't help but glance to my side, first my right, then my left, then up.

"You hear them too? You do, I know you do," the man said, pointing his finger, accusing me.

"They're in here. Voices. Somes real clear like the boy, like your mom. That's right. She's talking to me now. Saying things like she never had a chance with you. Like you will love her. Like she wants you to join her. I hear her voice and understand. But other voices are just tiny bits of dirt in a pile so they all get mashed together. And now you're trapped here with them. Trapped real good."

"I'm not trapped. You can't keep me here. I'll get out."

"You trapped alright, but I will be the one to get you out, no worries. There's always a way out if you just look in the right place. Especially since you are just a piece of me, and we got some different ways me and you. Let me tell you a story about me, since you're home with me now."

He held a finger in the air, and I clenched on to the book, listening to him but ready to smash it on his head if he got too close.

"My dad was the real devil, you see. An animal-hurting, Jervis-beating red devil. And God Damn he loved the H just like you do. Except he went to jail all the time, you see. I was always in hospitals for being crazy and he always went to jail, until the fucker finally died in jail. I didn't know until I saw the box of his remains when they sent them home. Moms always wanted him to die, but I think she was mad she wasn't the one who killed him.

"'Your dad died and left me with a piece of shit car, a bottle of ashes, and you,' she said, and made me and my dad's ashes stay downstairs. So I stayed down there, but I'd come up and steal from her all the time. Stole her money, her jewelry. Whatever. Pawned stuff. All for some H. Always coming back to the basement to get high. Living was good.

"But my moms had enough. She locked me down there one day. Banged the door shut with nails. Gave me a bucket to piss in and told me she'd let me out in three days after the poison was out of me. Three days in my own fucking tomb. I pounded on the door for hours. I called her names, I told her I would kill her when I got out. It didn't work. I was so far gone I wanted to scratch and claw out every bit of my cramping skin. I couldn't.

"The voices came back to me. It was my own skin cells talking to me. They were butchering each other. Sucking the marrow out of each other like little cannibals since I had no H to feed them. The darkest pain was in my back. It was like black burning liquid was boiling inside. It was torture…"

His words faded off and so did his gaze. The man wasn't even looking at me anymore but up and to the right, like he was staring through the walls to space. He barely knew I was there. I could hear his breath, like his nose was broken, and I clenched my hands on to the pile of clothes I was sitting on. I grasped the book, and waited to scream if I heard a car door slam outside.

"But I was not through. I searched the basement for hours to find something to get me high. Everywhere. Anything to stop the pain. A half a Vic. A roach of a joint. Nothing. The place felt like a grave, and I just wanted to die in it. Just me and dad's ashes.

"So I took him out.

"You see, when I was high I would play with dad. I would pour him on the table and push the piles into little mountains, knock them back down again, all to see what he was made of. My red-devil dad shot more dope than anybody we know. When I looked at those grey ashy lines, I thought, *maybe there is enough dope burnt out of his body to get me by.* That's what I thought for the longest time, how much smack has been left in those ashes.

"And then I heard it. I heard his voice, like an old man's whisper. 'SON,' he said, 'YOU NEED SOMETHING TO FIX WITH. SHOOT SOME.'

"I was crazy, see, crazy as I am now and crazy as you will always be. But the grey seemed to rise in the air and speak to me.

"'ASHES OF BURNT UP SMACK. GO AHEAD, BOIL IT AND FIX UP.'

"Bullshit, I thought, of course, but he kept talking, saying over and over, 'BOIL IT AND FIX UP.'

"Maybe there is dope left in there, I thought.

"'THERE IS. THERE IS,' he said.

"Where else would it go? I thought.

"'IT'S HERE.' He told me.

"No time for cotton filter or none of that shit that me and you don't use anyways. This was my dad. Fuck you Mom, I thought, fuck you. I boiled it up.

"It was chunky in the syringe and dark oil in the barrel, but I hit the vein. And ahhh yes. It was like an angel had come to me. Like every cell that was butchering my insides had laid down its knives and the smooth warmness was around me again. You see what I mean? The ashes were an army and fought back the evil sickness that had invaded my body down there. I could see the dark ashes travel through my veins. I could see them good as you can see your own veins."

He put a finger on me. I flinched, thought about punching him, but instead just listened.

"I felt so god damned blessed then like I was sprouting wings my own damn self. Best milk-blood you ever had. Music filled the basement the days I was down there, like a nice violin with my veins as strings. I shed my old skin and grew a new one. When my moms finally ripped out the nails, opened the door, and came down…well, she saw what I was, and…I ain't gonna scare you with that story, but she never bothered me again. I became a Red-Man.

"So now I do things. I do lots of things. One of them's filling me up with the right kinds of people, and the other is filling peoples up with the right parts of me. I been changed forever. That's how you got in your momma, and that's how come you're like me.

"And before I take you out to the back yard to be back with your momma, I think you need a little bit of me in your veins. You need it. You'll see."

The bedside story was over. I pushed myself farther back away from him and imagined paths out of the room. He stood tall in front of me, and pulled a syringe out of his pocket like a magician waving a magic wand. He uncapped it, and I heard a *pop*. He aimed it under his neck and looked like one of those people who puts a gun up against their chin pretending they're going to shoot, only he did shoot. He poked the needle right into himself.

His body jerked. My muscles clenched. He was pulling down on the plunger, yanking as if the needle was stuck. He started grunting, his face twisted up. I had my chance. *Stay small, quick, and zip.* I started my dash off the bed.

One step, two steps, and I was past him to the door. "Vermicious," he yelled, and swiped his leg under mine. I went sprawling sideways and landed on the wooden ground. Dust and dirt flew up, got on my tongue and in my eyes. I started to spit and got up to dash again when he grabbed me with one hand, and tossed me back on the bed.

"You're not done here? Never done here. I told you. You're made from me and the same as me. Same veins from my dad are in you. I will show you what else you can shoot, not just the H. You're my girl. Once you taste this, you'll see."

He grabbed me then, and pulled my arm and clamped it to his side. His tentacle fingers squeezed my hand so tight, trying to get me to be still. I could hear my bones crinkle. He was going to poke me with the rusty syringe. I punched his back with my free hand and screamed "NO" a hundred times. None of it mattered. He was a big hulk of a being.

My breath was leaving me. My heart thumped waiting to explode out of my chest. I was going to die here and wanted to. I didn't want anything like this inside of me. I wanted to be back at home, in bed, back at school eating lunch, back at recess, with my back against the wall with boys teasing me and me teasing back. Isn't someone supposed to be here at times like these?

I felt the tiny prick of the needle hit my skin, like stepping on a pin and you can't pull away. It was over.

A smashing noise from outside of the house shattered the air of the room. It felt like an alarm, and it woke me into hope. The Red-Man stopped everything. The sound of a car door slamming, two car doors, then more. Then voices followed. Murmurs. Like men getting ready for work. Or somebody getting ready to save me.

He let go of my arm and I felt blood seep back into my skin. Louder steps came from the front of the house. Was this real or just another one of the sounds this house makes? The Red-Man wasn't sure either. He was confused, I could tell. He wasn't the master anymore.

We heard footsteps, chatter, movement, and I waited for the right moment to scream. The noises got closer. Someone shouted from the front door;

"Hello. Hello. Hello in there!" the voice boomed serious like an assistant principal. "Attention. Heads up. Here ye, and pay attention all you mother fuckers….you have five minutes to vacate. Five minutes. This house is being secured and boarded up, and you can't squat here no more if that's what you been doing. We are armed. We will let you leave. Leave now. Leave now. Leave now, now, now. Leave now, now…"

He started humming and singing. I could hear his feet moving along as if he was dancing to his own words. "Attention: I repeat. Attention, attention. If anyone is in here, you must leave now. This home is going dark. You got four minutes to leave….da doo doo da doo doo" he hummed to himself.

The Red-Man kept his grip on me but his heart seemed to drop to the floor. I was going to be free. "HELP…" I started to scream, when his hand clamped over my mouth and cut the scream short.

"Don't you say a word," he whispered in my ear so close I could feel his breath fill my ear canal. "You're staying here, you see. We just gonna hide and let them board it all up."

His hand was stuffed over my mouth and I could taste the skin between my lips. Salty, dirty. He dragged me across the room and pulled me into a closet, but it had no doors.

Stuffed in the corner, in a closet, but not hidden. They should find us. They will find us if they look, they had to, right?

"Come out, come out if you in there. We don't want to chase you out."

"Shhhhh," the Red-Man whispered to me. We heard their boots inside the house, not moving fast, not moving deep. Just standing at the front. Shuffling. Waiting.

The smell of the Red-Man's breath filled the closet, and I couldn't help but breathe it deep into my nose since my mouth was covered. I could tell his heart was beating hard and his pulse was racing. My own heart thumped in my chest and banged against my chest bones. My body felt so weak like it was disintegrating, like I was turning to ash too and would scatter in the air.

Boots paced a bit. The sound of men working, some grunts. Objects being moved. They were smoking. The smell of freshly lit cigarettes mixed in with the burnt scents of old.

"You got one minute now. One minute mother fuckers. Gather up your shit and go. We starting with the windows now, then the door closes. Closes, closes, closes."

"It's empty, let's just get this done," said a brand new voice.

"Maybe upstairs. Maybe down. Go look," said another.

"Fuck that. The pounding will make anyone leave if they're in here. Come on, its late," and then more shuffling.

I pictured what was about to happen. This place would go from dark grey to full black. Thick dark black, like being buried alive. Then what? The others in the basement. They'd come up. The voices. The boy. They'd come in. It would be like a dark cemetery and I would be the only one alive inside. Nobody from the street would hear me scream. Who will look for me? My dad? Someone from school?

The man's hand was still stuffed in my mouth. I had a plan.

I let my lips part and opened my jaws wide. His fingers slipped inside my mouth, and I snapped my teeth shut and squeezed my jaw hard as I could. My teeth sunk into his fingers like I was a rabid pit bull. I felt bone, tasted salt and grime and all the dirt of this floor. I didn't stop but kept clenching like a stray dog. Blood from his finger was on my lips. He screamed in anger and shock, jerked up in reflex, and pushed me away shouting nasty cusses just for woman.

I was halfway out the room from his push, and kept on running. I was free, and dashed down the hallway. I saw the light of the front door, and the shadows of men standing still. I didn't want to stop, but scurried right by them like a rat running across the floor. They didn't seem too surprised to see me. But I was gone.

I thought they might follow me but they stayed inside. I was just a little creature in their big world. Two of their trucks were parked in front, and my dad's car was parked across the way. The outside air was the color of dusk, but everything was just like I left it. I bounced up the front steps of my house, and then turned for a last glimpse. I saw the Red-Man. He wasn't chasing me. He was walking around the front door, trying to carry a bunch of stuff. He dropped it on the ground, tried to pick it back up, and then dropped it again.

The man couldn't live there anymore. He would need to go somewhere else, but I was back where I lived and safely inside.

* * *

"You let her go. Why? You had her and didn't bring her to me."

"I am done. I am leaving here. Men are here."

"I will go to her. I will get her myself."

"I shall get her first and make her mine."

Chapter Eleven: Lilly Back Home

I lay underneath my familiar blanket but it never felt as strange as this. Cars drove by and their headlights reflected though my bedroom window and made shadows move across the room. I watched them go from left to right across my wall, sometimes fast, sometimes slow. Sometimes noisy engines seemed like they would crash right through the brick right into my bedroom.

I was panting and sweating when I first escaped the Red-Man and made it back into my house. I tossed my backpack on the ground, and was going to run into my dad's arms and tell him everything. That all changed the minute I saw him.

His angry eyes made me freeze. Something else was happening.

The lady from child protective service came to our house today. She was with someone. They looked around. Looked in my bedroom. Looked in our refrigerator. Asked my Dad questions.

"They are on me again because of you. That's why you were staying away from home after school today isn't it?" Dad said, but he didn't really want me to answer. All I could hear was Grandma smacking her lips like she was drinking Ensure. The chocolate flavor.

"What you been telling people? You know you don't talk about our business. They'll take you away to somewhere else and you'll never see me again? You want that I guess. They're coming back here again and if I don't do the whole list they gave me then guess what? You gone."

I could have told him right then about the Red-Man. I could have shown him the scrapes on my arms for proof. Maybe he would stop being mad at me and just kill the man across the street. He would kill him, I knew it. Especially since he had that smell on him from getting drunk. But I wasn't sure I wanted that. The Red-Man said a lot of things. He had answers to questions that my dad wouldn't tell me.

I felt restless and couldn't sleep. My skin felt clammy, and I knew it was from not having the medicine. I was safe in my own bed at least. I had Chef Boyardee ravioli for dinner, but then had diarrhea right after that. Now I felt all empty inside. My nose was runny, and I kept wiping it on my pajama sleeve. The pajamas were dirty anyways. I wished he'd wash them because that was when they were my favorite, right after they were out of the dryer.

The protective service lady taking me away? What would that be like? I thought of being in a new house with a new family, trapped again, like I was across the street. The house was all boarded up, for now at least, like a person tied-up with gags in its mouth. It is the Red-Man who needed to go somewhere else, not me. I wanted to stay with my dad and Grandma in my own house.

Dad had Grandma in the bath, and my bedroom door was cracked open so that I could hear the splashes. I couldn't sleep. Today was a bad day and not over, and I wanted someone to help me. Someone who really was protective services.

I lay there for a long time, watching headlight shadows on the wall. After a while, Dad came into my room. He had a steamy cloud from the bath around him and smelled of soap and anger. I knew he was holding it in. If he knew everything, he would probably explode.

"You still awake Lill'? Go to sleep. I'll drive you to school tomorrow. I'll make you lunch. We'll talk. We have to get the next few days exactly right."

He was taking me to school. I had planned to say I was too sick to go, but if he was driving me, maybe it would be okay. We could talk. I wanted him to stay and talk to me now.

"Dad, how long is Grandma going to live here?" I ask this a lot.

"Long as she is alive she is gonna stay with me."

"How long is that?"

"Grandma is going to live forever," he said. But I know he didn't mean it.

"Ciana likes to call her a witch. Maybe that's why."

"Kids say a lot of things, they joking."

I thought of the way Grandma's skin sags on her neck and the way she smells when I lie next to her. It made me feel safe, but it wasn't what a person should smell like. Plus, Grandma didn't even know who I was sometimes. Most times. A witch would always know. Ciana shouldn't be so scared.

"If I had a mommy, I would take care of her forever, like you do."

"You do have a mom, we all have them. You just don't see yours."

Because I was sick. That's why she left, I wanted to say. Mothers don't stick around for blue veiny sick children.

"When will we be with Mommy again? Is that still never?"

"Someday," my dad said and looked away. "You do the best with what you got. Do the best with what you got. That's what we do. But some just don't understand that."

I felt my back ache and the scrapes on my arm burned. My muscles were still bunching up and turning on me, begging me to help them. They seemed to be whispering, *We could have had the needle today, why not?*

"Daddy, I'm still sick, do they have to cut me again?"

"Doctors always trying to cut you. We're doing okay. They said you wouldn't even be here now. But look at you, look at me. Don't you ever believe anything that comes in your ears you know in your heart isn't right. That's how we got here. Now good night."

He kissed me on the forehead and then my cheeks, and I still felt the gruff of his whiskers on my skin when he left. The bedroom door he left open, just a crack, and a ray of the hallway light shot into the room. Across my room, my closet door was open, and the dark shadows came to life. I needed to get up and close the closet door. I hated it being open, and it reminded me of the dark closet from across the street.

Then I heard a voice.

"Lilly."

I searched inside me to see if it was coming from my own body or not.

"Lilly."

"Lilly."

God I hope I don't have to go to the hospital tonight. The nurses would see the scrapes. There would be more questions. I would be taken away.

"Lilly"

"What, what?" I finally answered.

"You want to play. Do you play with anybody?"

I turned my head and was eye to eye with the red stuffed bear. The one I got for winning tickets at the pizzeria. The stuffing was all smashed down and the neck of the bear couldn't hold the head up anymore but just limped to one side no matter how I set it on the pillow.

I watched it closer to see if the lips moved. They didn't. It couldn't talk, that would be impossible, but it did turn its head, even with a broken neck, and the marble black eyes looked at me.

"Do you play with anybody?" The voice asked again, and I knew who it was. The boy from across the street, speaking in just a whisper.

"I don't play with anybody," I said, barely with my lips but mostly in my head.

"I don't either. We can play."

I thought of screaming and then saying I needed to go to the hospital. Dad would be so mad. He wouldn't know what to do with Grandma. He would drive too fast and the car seats would be cold. He'd smoke in the car. The car would 'ding' because he wouldn't wear his seatbelt.

Or I could just listen to this boy talk, safe in my own bed.

"Okay, we can play, but you aren't real."

"I am real. I live across the street. You know that. You were here. You are my friend."

"You don't even know me."

"Yes, I know you have a purple backpack. I know you wear blue pants to school usually and a white shirt…I know your daddies. Both of them."

"How do you know?"

"I know because I see them," the boy's whisper said. "And I know because I know your mom."

This was a bad joke.

I traced my fingertip along the sewed up linings of the red bear to see if the stuffing was falling out. Outside the door, I heard echoes of water splashing from the bathtub and my dad pacing back and forth.

"How do you know her?"

"We're together now. She has been here for a while. I been here longer."

"How did you get inside my house?"

"Through the sewer line. Under the street. We can't stay too long. It's not easy. I can't explain it. You'll see what I mean if you come back here with me."

"I can't go back there. It's not safe."

"Come back here for me Lilly. Please. I need you to help me…"

His voice faded. I didn't know if I needed more of the H or if it was the smack that was making these voices, but I was pretty sure that the pinch of the needle in my arm would make all of this go away.

"Lilly," a voice came again. This time from the other side.

"Lilly."

It was a woman. I turned my head at the sound of the voice. Yes, it was a woman, but she was older, and her voice was harsh, like someone who smoked too many cigarettes.

"Lilly, that's what he calls you. It is a nice name. A flower of death and new beginnings."

"Who are you?"

"I am your mother."

Poison blood bubbled in my heart. My lungs couldn't get enough air and I gasped for breath. My skin turned a paler shade of blue.

"No, you left me. Why are you here?"

"I did leave. I'm sorry. I was afraid you were evil."

"Maybe I am."

This wasn't my mom. This was the sick part of me that needed medicine. I could feel the atoms of my body tingling, separating from one another, and then all of them began to fight. It started a war with fiery explosions in my gut. Lava climbed up my throat.

"Where are you?" I asked, but not ready to trust the answer.

"Close by. Where you were today. I have always been here. Do you want to come to me?"

"Yes, I think so, but dad said you were far."

"No, I am not. He put me close to you."

"He put you somewhere?"

"Ask him when you can. Where he buried me."

Dad was in the bath with his own mother, cleaning her, keeping her safe. He took care of the women in his life. That's all he does. He would take care of my mom, too. Something wasn't right.

"If you are my mom for real, then can I see you?"

"Yes, I will try to get you. To bring you to me. I hope it works so I don't have to kill you."

"Why would you kill me?"

"So they will bury you with me. Somehow we will be together again. Me inside you, or you next to me."

"Just stay here if you are really my mom. I am sick and need someone."

She said nothing to that. I curled up in a ball and spread my fingers across my stomach trying to calm down the fire inside that was brewing. It didn't work. Acid was burning up my insides, and the fire sent gross stuff up my esophagus like it was a dirty chimney. Muscles cramped, and my brain was confused.

"I have to go," She said.

"Don't go."

"It's okay. Someone will come to you soon. I have arranged it."

"Where are you going?"

"Your dad killed me, so I will kill his mom."

Chapter Twelve: Zach the Caretaker

"The bathroom is a most dangerous place. People slip and fall and shatter their hips. Or they grab sharp objects and cut themselves. Or they drown in water that is too hot and scolds their skin or is too cold and gives hyperthermia. Or they overdose on medications with labels too tiny to read. The bathroom is a slaughterhouse. You need to be careful there."

The home health care nurse had said this to Zachary more than once. She spoke it with rhythm, as if she were a poet in a poetry slam, and made sure Zach felt it and wouldn't forget. She said he had his hands full trying to take care of a young girl and an elderly woman at the same time. He called her a dumb fuck in response. She didn't come back after that.

It was too much for him, she was right, but fuck her and fuck protective service. He messed that up today too and he knew it. They said the same damn thing in a different way. "There is caregiver burnout," they had said, "which dulls the senses, makes you lose your empathy. You may unwillingly let those you love go uncared for. This can lead to tragedy we know you don't want. Adult protective service will also be contacted to see how they can help."

More people are coming, is what they really were telling him. He swore at them with drunken breath, and then emptied the 100 proof vodka bottle when they left. He had another bottle waiting. They left him with an "action plan." This wasn't for his protection—this was their way of swearing back at him with orders and threats. What they hell do they know?

His mom was safe and strong, but possibly delirious. Who knew what she would say when they talk to her. Zach had his own action plan, though, and he would see it through. Tomorrow was the first day of the month. He'd get his mom's disability check and new food stamp money. If he acted fast enough, he could get groceries, clean the house, and be ready for their next visit.

He took a drink straight from the freezer-chilled vodka bottle, and listened to the humming noise his mom made in the bath. He knew the warm water soothed her. She would sway her arms to and fro and make tiny splashes that echoed in the shallow "impossible-to-drown-in" bath water. He was just steps away putting Lilly to sleep. Lilly might be spending her last night here if he didn't do things right. Protective services was setting him up to make taking her away easy, but he wouldn't let that happen.

"If I had a mommy, I would take care of her forever, like you do," Lilly had said, and later asked that same question she has been asking for years; "When will we be with mommy again? Is that still never?"

It was never, he had told her that long ago, but didn't want to repeat it. Lilly could never find out that if her mother had her way, she wouldn't even be alive but would have died at one month old. But somehow it was Zach who was the one *not fit to be a full time caregiver.* That's what the people with suits and badges said. That he should only be allowed to take care of Lilly if a fulltime nurse was there to take care of her grandmother. Well, who's going to pay for that?

He wished he could give Lilly answers when she asked about her mom. He wished he could say something like, *your mommy will always be your mommy and you can have your mommy forever. You and me are like that. We both love our mommies.* But she needed to know she could live without a mother. Without him even. She wasn't like a regular kid. She was blue, and he loved that about her, loved that her insides came out, but she wasn't built for this world. At least not this street. He needed to give her a strong suit of armor that would protect her forever.

So he lied and said "some day" and figured she'd learn to live with hopes unfulfilled and dreams being dashed. *Do the best you can with what you got.* That was what mattered.

He kissed her on the forehead and both cheeks, like a priest giving the sign of the cross. Her bedroom was dark, and he could see how it was both peaceful and terrifying. Soft stuffed animals lined the walls like a pink friendly posse, but in the dark they seemed to come alive.

Doors opened just a crack in this house. That's how he survived, and the bathroom door was the same. The warm octave of splashing sounds bounced off the bathroom walls. Time to check in on her.

"Get out of here. I'm naked. Get out."

"Ma, it's me, your son."

"Jeffrey? Jeffrey!"

She was bathing in hot water and talking out of dementia, and now he knew it would be that way until morning. He didn't deny being Jeffrey. He let her believe that he was her deceased husband—especially at times like this, when she was exposed.

Her body in the bath seemed more like a carcass and ceased being a body long ago. The shell she was in had melted, like it was wax, and drip, drip, dripped into something that seemed embalmed already, but her spirit was way too strong to leave it. At times he almost admired the leathery resolve of her body and the lines that had become so rich over the years. He could see his own childhood inside the crevices of her skin.

How many times had he taken a lickin for Momma? Got in Dad's face, or pissed him off on purpose? A few. His brother took more, though, before he finally whipped Dad's ass, but now he was in the penitentiary for home invasion. They shipped him to Indiana, too far to travel to, so now they just delivered a Christmas present and sent a few bucks for the commissary. Another brother was dead at the age of 14. Shot by a policeman. Three brothers, two gone, and just him and Nelson now. But memories of days when they were all together lived on with this ancient woman in the tub. Playing baseball, sneaking into concerts, smoking weed and sharing headphones. They were tight before things fell apart.

He touched the bath water expecting it to feel warm, but instead it was cold as pond water. It was time to get her out.

"Ma, let's pull the drain."

She lay there on her back with her head flat on the drain and her eyes staring upwards. The bath water was soapy but he could see she had urinated by the milky yellow clouds.

"Mom, let's get you out of there now."

"Don't touch me," she said, and took a swing at his hand but missed.

"Can you pull yourself up then?"

"No, damn it, it's sucking me down."

"What?"

"The bathtub is eating me, Jeffrey. It started to eat me."

He felt the back of her head, and some of her hair was indeed down the drain. He pulled on the hair gently, expecting it to give, but nothing. His fingers slipped along the wet strands that were stuck.

"My son, Zachary. He did this. He left me in the cold water. He left me in here and killed his baby's momma and buried her body. He's no good and now I'm dead."

"I'll take care of this, Ma. Don't worry. Don't say that."

Why they hell would she say that? Zach wondered. *She heard the detectives asking me questions. Must be.*

No, she is a witch and knows all.

"It's ripping me, Jeffrey. Pulling my hair."

"It's your son's fault. He's not fit to be a god-damned caregiver," Zach said, hoping it would make her stop screaming. His mom had no memory of her husband Jeffrey dying. How his esophageal varices exploded from alcoholism and he bled out on the carpet. Zach rolled up and threw away the carpet that the dead body lay on.

"It's got me. It's got me. I'm cold. I'm naked. Jeffrey, help me and stop being so rotten."

The drain was probably backed up again. He may have to go downstairs and undo an elbow and snake it. Damn thing was always backing up from Lilly's hair and leaking into the basement. Crazy black gook inside the pipe had to be poked through with a clothes hanger.

Zach took a huge slug of the vodka, felt it tug at his throat, but his body needed something else. He needed more to get through this night.

"I can get it, Ma. Just please stay still."

"Don't touch me. I'm naked Jeffrey. It's ripping my hair out of my head."

He put a hand under her neck, grasped the wet, slimy hair, and pulled up.

Nothing. It wouldn't budge. *Should have gotten her a haircut.* It was wet and thin. His hands tried to grasp around the tiny spine of her neck and pull, but it felt like it would snap if he tried. He could feel her life flowing through the vertebrate.

"I'm freezing cold. My hair is being ripped. It's getting inside my head and ripping at my brain."

He imagined how shriveled her body would get if she were in the water any longer, like it was being soaked in formaldehyde. He kept poking and prying with his fingers trying to feel where her hair was stuck. With his pinky he could feel the drain sucking like a vacuum cleaner, and her hair was being trapped with the gook.

"Stop killing me."

This had to end soon.

Then he heard a new voice.

"Daddy, you're being loud. I'm scared."

It was Lilly. He turned to see her standing there, holding on to her red teddy, with her eyes squinting from the bathtub light. She was half asleep, but the stuffed animal was looking much more awake and perky. He wanted to yell at her to get back to bed, but then stopped. *We have to get through these next few days exactly right.* Child protective services. Adult protective services. They were swarming this house soon, and this moment would come up during interviews.

"This man is killing me," his mom's voice echoed from the bathtub.

"Lilly, she's just having some problems in the tub. Lay in bed and count to 50 and I should be there."

"I'll be dead," said his mom.

"Maybe count twice, Lilly. I'm sorry. We can sleep in tomorrow and I'll take you to breakfast and drive you to school and you can even be late."

She shuffled back into her room without a word, and he looked back down at his mom's skeletal body. Tiny drops of water dripped in pairs of two from the bathtub faucet. Drip-drop, drip-drop. If she were here for a year or more, it would fill up and she'd drown.

But he'd have her out in a few minutes. He would just cut some of her hair. Three snips and it would be over. Both his mom and child would be sleeping peaceful and clean. Both of them.

He grabbed some tiny scissors out of the medicine cabinet. The metal on the scissors were dark yellow and rusty but would do. He put his fingers in the scissor loops and turned ready to cut her out, but when he did, she screamed. She howled. It was so loud he thought something in the tub had bitten into her, but no, it was himself that she was afraid of.

"I'm just going to cut one or two hairs to get you out, Ma."

More screams. Her body shook and spasmed like he had thrown a toaster into the tub, but only her head was partly stuck and couldn't move much. He waited to see if she'd rip herself out, but she didn't. More thrashing.

"You're gonna hurt yourself, Ma. Just stop it."

She wasn't able to hear. He thought of slapping her. He thought of leaving and coming back when she calmed down. He thought of pouring vodka in her throat. Instead, he put the scissors on the counter and flipped back thru the medicine cabinet: Advil. Tylenol PM. Tums. Toothpaste tube with no cap and a ball of hardened toothpaste at the top. Prescriptions bottles. That was the real gold. Especially the Xanax.

But how many? She rarely took it, he was the only one who gobbled them as needed. The label was faded, but it was Xanax he was quite sure. The white 2 mg bars that he knew so well felt familiar in his fingers. He popped three pills into his own mouth just to make sure. He needed them tonight. They will mellow him down before he blew up.

But I've been drinking. Last time I mixed alcohol and Xanax, I went completely crazy. A boy died.

Just don't leave the house tonight, he told himself, just finish this and be done.

He popped another Xanax in his mouth, and then grabbed three more pills between his fingers. In one fluid motion he reached down and slipped them through the crack of his mother's lips, gently using his thumbs to slide them deep into her throat. Her tongue felt like a slug. Her mouth tried to reject the pills but couldn't. Gags and screeches echoed off the bathroom tile and ricocheted back and forth. He had made her sound like a witch. All these years and he had done that to her.

But he had too, right? He was just glad his thumb down her throat didn't make her puke. He cupped some water from the faucet, placed it on her tongue, and waited. She lapped a bit, then coughed, but it brought up nothing. All of the Xanax went down. Both of them would be calm soon and figure this out.

"Get me up. It's pulling on me, pulling on me, it's ripping my brain out."

Every word was getting sharper. The high pitch shrieks started to stab into his stomach. It wasn't really *ripping her brain out,* he knew that. Mom had exaggerated everything since he was a little boy. She used to tell him to be ready for her funeral. That she was sick and dying. That she had a disease from all the hurt inside. He got used to acting like he believed her. And still today people in his life are always saying they were going to die, always saying they needed a doctor or a hospital. He knew what death looked like better than the doctors did. He'd had as many people die at his hands as the damn doctors. Mom wasn't dying in this tub. She was still trying to be a puppet master and control people, but not anymore. Latrice was a puppet master, too. Oh, God could she get in people's heads, until he put her down.

He left his mom alone but kept the door open a crack. Her murmurs faded and lightly echoed like they were far away. He peeked into Lilly's room. She was awake. Muttering things, but okay and in bed. His life was full of cracked doors. He needed a shot. He cracked open his second bottle of chilled, 100 proof vodka. First shot out of a bottle is always the strongest, and it burned like gasoline in his throat.

He went downstairs to the basement and the smell of sewage and mold hit him. The air was humid, and scents stuck to his skin. Dirty laundry was piled in one corner, and the furnace seemed to ignite as a greeting. It rattled like a drunk man in armor.

He stepped over the piles and stood below the bathtub. A bucket remained on the ground from times before when he had to unscrew the pipes, scrape away at the hair, and unclog the drain from the hairy gook. It still leaked. He looked up at the bathtub pipes, and was surprised he couldn't hear his mom. At least not her words. She was splashing about in the water but the screaming had stopped.

She would be mellow soon. The Xanax wasn't for lightweights. He'd done as much himself, and it froze his brain and all the nerves in his body. *Except if you drink on it, you stay awake and lose control. You black out and firebomb houses and little kids die.*

Get this done, then lie in bed, he told himself. He wasn't going to fuck this up. He had to do things perfect this week.

At least it was quiet down here, underneath the earth. Up above they waited for him to take care of things. His two girls, one who was family, and the other who he agreed to father ever since he put her mother down. He'd signed up that day to do everything for her, but now they said it wasn't enough.

Fuck it. He should just stay here in the quiet underworld. This is where his brother Nelson came to escape sometimes and fix up with his dope. Used syringes in shoeboxes were left behind like animal tracks.

But he acted, like he always did, and reached up to unscrew the elbow that lead to the bathtub drain and always leaked.

The elbow was an old, plastic-to-galvanized-steel connector. He had to stand on a block of wood and stretch up as high as he could to reach it. He felt his arms ache. They were aging arms, like this damn pipe. Everything was getting older and the rust was showing.

He twisted it open and got ready for a splash of water to drip into the bucket, but none came. The drain was still closed. Clogged. A bunch of hair and dirt and soapy grime was now filling the pipe. He grabbed a metal clothes hanger, straightened out the tip, and poked upward.

He hit something, he felt it, not something solid, but something squishy. The clothes hanger got stuck in the muck. He pulled back on it, and a darky gooey liquid trickled down the pipe. Tiny drops hit the bucket.

A scream echoed from upstairs. No words, just something yelling in pain. He was not even sure if it was his mother. The pitch was way outside her range. What the fuck? He didn't poke her, did he? There was something squishy blocking the pipe.

"Daddy, daddy, where are you? Come here, come here fast."

Lilly. Goddamn it, she was awake. His face burned with heat. His body raged against the house, this street, this universe. He couldn't take it. He needed help. Get me a damn home health care nurse or nanny and fuck the insurance company bullshit. He rehearsed his talk with all of them in his head—Medicaid, protective service, social security disability, and all the rest as he dashed up the stairs, taking them two at a time. The booze and Xanax fueled him.

Upstairs in the hallway, he saw both Lilly's door and the bathroom door were wide open. He turned the corner and there was Lilly kneeling down by the tub. Her pajamas were wet and her face was full of tears. Her sobs whined in a helpless plea.

She was trying to pull her Grandma out of the bath, or at least what was left of her Grandma. Inside the bath was something Zach couldn't recognize.

Sludge and gunk had wrapped itself all around his mother's head. The hair from the drain had moved and was now all over her face. It had gotten into her mouth, into her nostrils, covered up most of her cheeks. She was still and lifeless, but the whites of her eyes peeked out. The eyes were blank, but she was alive and breathing. Just giving the Xanax stare.

Zach moved Lilly aside with force and reached into the tub. He yanked this time at his mother's head with all his might, and right away her head was lifting up. The hair was stretching like taffy. He grasped his mom's head as if it were a barbell and he was doing a curl. He grunted and felt his whole bicep engage.

Lilly stepped back, sat in the corner, but was watching. He needed to make this right. Oh fuck, why is she stuck and he needed to call 911. But then cops would come and protective service would know and he was already drunk with a swirling head that was about to blow.

But it was giving. Long stretches of hair that weren't even hers were being pulled from the drain. His mom's body was nearly fully sitting up, and her neck tilted forward but still attached to the sludge. Was she breathing? Was her heart beating? Was it just the Xanax that put her out?

One more tug and it would break free. The whole big patch of it seemed to be sliding up the pipes. It wouldn't be much longer. His mom would be free and he'd clean her up and put her down to bed.

More tugs and grunts and *SPLOT*—the whole thing popped from the drain.

His mom was out and free. The gunk of hair was in his fist, and out of the sewer line attached to the handful of hair he held so tight was the head of Latrice. His infection. Lilly's mother, was back.

Zach looked down at her face. Her flesh was like a corpse that had been in water and nibbled at by fish. Her cheek had melted away revealing her jaw, but her deep eyes and infectious glance was still present. The earrings he gave her 12 years ago were still attached—fake diamond studs. The lips he kissed were there but had shriveled, unmistakably hers. The same mouth he had put a pillow over until she died was moving.

Then the mouth spoke.

"Stop being so rotten Zachary. Why are you so rotten?"

The words mocked, they enraged. He felt steam shooting through him and with one hand grabbed the rusty scissors off the sink. He held Latrice's head up by a handful of her hair, and began puncturing.

"Stop being so rotten Zachary, stop being so rotten."

The words kept coming and echoed like a wicked parrot, and each time he heard it he stabbed the tiny pair of scissors into her head. He sliced her cheeks, the sides of her neck, into her eyes especially—he needed to dot out those eyes. The last time he saw them was at her death, and this time he poked them right out until they were mush. The rusty metal scissors sliced and diced.

When his roars of rage died down, Lilly was in the corner of the bathroom, rolled up into a ball with her hands over her eyes.

And in the tub was her Grandma. Her body was limp. Her hair swayed in the water that had now turned red as if tomato paste. And her face was pecked apart like a scarecrow that the birds no longer feared. Her eyes were fully gone, having been punctured a dozen or more times, and much of the flesh had been ripped off her face. Stabs into her neck made blood flow like a waterfall into the bath water.

There was no sign of anything else. No Latrice. No dismembered head—only a dead, old woman bathing in her own blood.

What happened?

"You seen that? You seen that? You seen that right Lilly? You seen what I seen?"

Chapter Thirteen: Lilly and the Day Everything Changed

"You seen that? You seen that? You seen that right, Lilly? You seen what I seen?"

His voice had that rage which dared me to even think different. I needed to stay still and agree or he'd be angry and hurt someone else. I could feel it. Don't say much, don't admit any truths. And don't look down and to the left when you talk. I did not see whatever it was he was talking about.

"Yes, Poppa, I saw it."

Poppa. I said Poppa. I hadn't said Poppa in years, but why did I say that? And what did he see that I hadn't? I had covered my eyes with my hands as soon as I saw him swing the scissors at Grandma. When I had opened them, I wished I hadn't. My grandma was in a bath of her own blood, and her eyes were still open and staring at the ceiling. Her mouth was open, too, like it was stuck in a scream. And my dad had killed her.

"It was her, Lilly. It was your momma. Your momma was here. In the bath"

All I could see was mushy stuff all over Grandma's face. Her body was floating in the bloody mess of the bathtub and her skin was changing colors.

My dad put his hands in the bath searching frantically under the water. Her body moved about, dead as a floating log, and tiny waves of blood bounced against the side of the tub.

"You saw her, you saw it. You did, right? Where did it go? Where did it go?"

Dead. He murdered her, and he was my crazy dad now. I hated when he talked like this. When he smelled like this. Like he was full of drunkenness and anger. The craziness spun around him, and his words starting spinning in a whirl that I was getting caught up in. Everything was changing for good tonight. I wrapped my arms around my gut, clenched each muscle, and waited for it to end.

"The head. It's here. In this house. What's happening? I have to see. You have to see. You don't know how this works. You burn and bury but maybe not. Maybe I did it wrong. Maybe she got out."

His words smelled of his insides. Grandma was dead and my insides were dying too. If I could see them, I am sure my insides would look like the bathtub looked.

"I got to find it. I didn't do this. This isn't real. Space is lost, time will come back. You stay here. Stay right here. Stay here. Stay."

I sat perfectly still, and looked up at him with an obedient nod. He darted out the door and I was left alone. His words hung in the air but his craziness left with him. I heard him rummaging through the garage and the clang of tools and clamoring of metal. This was bad.

Everything was falling apart.

I sat in stillness with Grandma. Not a sound, just my heart thudding, and once in a while a drop of water from the faucet. Drip, drop, with long pauses in between. Grandma's body changed, greyed, and seemed gentle in the bath. It was sweet, even, the way her body floated in the tub. I felt like there was a peace right now that was better than what had just happened, and better than what was about to come. I was nestled small but secure in-between the wall and the toilet, just a turtle inside its shell.

Grandma needed me there with her, I think. Like one of those funeral homes were people go to see the body, but it was just me. Like I was the new woman of this block. I thought of reaching out to touch her, to try and hold her, but it would have felt wrong. She was so still. Perfect. Peaceful. Grandma had lived a long time, and to do that on this street meant she won. The street didn't get her. People here die all the time from guns when they are 20, or they go to jail for 30 days or to the hospital to get their legs amputated. Grandma has been through all that with her kids, her sons, and she survived.

Until now.

If Dad can do this to his own mom, what might he do to me? Whatever he did, I would take it like Grandma did. I was tired of my body and wanted it to change. I looked at the way the blood swirled out of her neck and made circles in the water, little traces, like watercolor paints. I didn't want that, but what was left for me here?

I sat and listened for an answer in the drips. They dripped like a clock that ticked too slow and didn't tell me much. Just a high-pitched dripping sound that filled my head and then echoed through my aching body before disappearing. Time ticked on that way. I was waiting for something to happen next, felt like I should get up and get help, but I couldn't. Nobody else can know my business. I can't tell them. If they try to take me away, it will be somewhere bad. And if they do it is my fault.

I don't know how long I waited, only that every other plan of doing something other than waiting was not going to work. With no H to make me feel love inside, with no real protective service, with nothing but my dad, I was here until he came back.

Finally, there was a whooshing sound from the front door opening, and then the pounding of my dad's feet rushing back to me. Something important was being delivered. His panting breath arrived before he did.

When he rounded the corner and stood at the door, I saw him with a shovel in one hand and his pants covered in mud. A trail of dirt followed him. He dropped the shovel, which clanked to the floor.

In his other hand was a round, grey rock, that he palmed like it was a basketball. He was too tired to speak, so both of us waited for him to catch his breath. I pulled my legs up into my chest and put my hands on my face. I was ready to cover my eyes again soon.

"You see this?" he yelled, and held up the rock. "I got it. It is here. We need to unburn the house and unbury the truth. It starts with the head."

He tossed the grey ball into the bathtub and it splashed near Grandma's feet, making waves in the red water.

My hands went over my eyes at first, afraid to see the truth he was telling me, but I spread my fingers apart and saw what it was. A skull. There was a skull floating in the bathtub, bobbing a bit, almost ready to come to rest.

It was not like one of those clean skulls you see for doctors to study, but an ashy grey one that looked part burnt up, part torn apart. Vacant eye sockets looked sideways and right at me.

"Lilly. That is your mother. I got her for you. See?" He pointed to the bathtub. "She's been dead. I can't tell you why. You don't need to know that. You only need to know she can't hurt you anymore. She wanted me to kill you, *to take care of you like I do*. Well, I did take care of you."

I tore off some toilet paper to rub the mucus and tears from my face, and I looked up at him. His voice sounded scared, loving, almost sweet, and unlike what I had ever heard. It was like I was looking at him as a five-year-old child, even though the lines on his face were deep and tired. There was danger in his eyes, but they weren't scary to me, they just looked damaged. I put a hand on his cheek. He was warm and clammy. Sweaty. Defective.

"She can't hurt you, see? If I had a mommy, I would take care of her like you do."

Dad was repeating what I had said to him in my bedroom. He remembered it. We stared at each other in the corner of the bathroom still thinking on these words when I heard someone else in the house. Someone with boots, and the steps got closer. Somebody was here and coming towards us, but my dad didn't seem to care, he stayed there kneeling in front of me, hypnotized or frozen. His sweat smelled of alcohol, but cold, like the outside air was still on him.

The noise of stomping boots got closer, and around the corner, I saw who it was. The Red-Man. He was here.

"You got things that are mine."

Dad's head turned, and he started to leap up, but the Red-Man was on the attack. He was holding a big piece of led pipe, and swung it with two hands at my dad in a baseball swing. By the time it crunched on my dad's head, I was back in my dark world behind my hands and fingers, not seeing but hearing the thwack.

"You got things that are mine." Another whack followed, but this one sounded like it hit his gut. "You ain't no Daddy, you see, and you got things that are mine."

My dad cursed, a long angry one, but it was cut short by a mushy thwack sound, and another, and another, until Daddy cursed no more. I heard a splash from the bath water and the Red-Man grunted and howled like a beast. I peeked between my fingers and there he was, my dad in the bath. His face was a mangled, purple mess and blood was gushing from his nose into the bath.

I couldn't hold back the tears at all this time. My eyes were puddles of mud.

Chapter Fourteen: Lilly Has To Go to the Basement

"They take my house, they take my family. They been taking things forever."

The Red-Man screamed this, but not at me, but at the pile of bodies in the bathtub. My father was on top, eyes closed, blood streaming from his nose into the water, and the side of his head bruised purple. His blood was thick, nearly chunky, not like Grandmas, which was thin as water. Grandma's skin was turning different shades of dark, like a grey rainbow, and at her feet was the skull. Just a part of what could be my mother.

I wasn't even sure if the Red-Man knew I was there until he turned to me

"Check date is tomorrow. I get money then but I need a house. A new one. Well, I'm taking this one. Burning down this house and then coming back to live here."

"Why? Why?" I cried. I couldn't believe I could even talk. My insides trembled like I was freezing to death.

"You let them board up my house and left me there. You ran from me. And this dad who says he's raising you. You call him Dad? You know he killed Oscar don't you know? Burned him right up. Reaping what he sowed. Getting what he deserves, you see. Everything is changing tonight."

He was right, and I knew that. Nothing would be the same.

"You, you have a choice. You can stay with me and burn it down, or I can do you like the others and put you in the basement. What will it be?"

"Don't touch me again. My uncle is next door. Police are coming. "

"Get to the basement. Get there now."

I would not go to the basement. I got up out of the corner and dashed by him. Where to run? I didn't know, so I grabbed the shovel in the doorway and swung it at the Red-Man. It made contact, right in the knee, and the metal gonged like it was a musical instrument. He cussed in pain. I was free.

I was quick to the front door. *Go to Nelson's. Someone will help. Go there.* My hand grasped the knob and started to spin. The door was locked. It wouldn't move. I twisted the lock with shaking hands and turned the handle again. The door opened. Fresh, cold air seeped in.

Slam.

The fresh air was cut right off. The Red-Man was behind me and his outstretched palm smashed into the door and forced it shut. I turned, looked up at his eyes, which already seemed to be on fire.

"The basement. Like Oscar, you're going down with this house. You can stay there forever, and talk to me from the ashes. Talk to me like Oscar."

He grabbed my arm and his skin burned hot. I tried to twist but couldn't. He was full of more anger and crazy than my dad ever was. By the time his other arm snagged me, all the twists and kicks with my legs to break free didn't matter.

The basement door was open and easy to find. He carried me there like a doll.

"After it burns, then we can talk."

He dropped me at the top of the stairs and slammed the basement door. I fell down one step and grabbed the handrail to not fall all the way. I waited there. I heard shuffling. I pushed the door back open and he slammed it shut again.

"You stayin in there. It's okay. Don't be scared of the basement."

I waited. Would he hurt me? Maybe not. He's crazy, and I can stay down here until daybreak. Protective service will come to save me, take me away to a new family. They will be here soon. Just one night in this dark, stinky basement. I can do that. When you get hurt this bad and scared like I am, something has to come in and save you, right? Both my parents are dead, that's why James had to escape in the peach.

I sat on the top stair and looked down. The staircase seemed like it was covered with bathtub blood. It felt like something down there was waiting for me. Breathing. Something that could only live in basements and wanted me with it. I hated it. Whenever I came down here, I'd just grab laundry off the pile quick as I could, turn off the light behind me, and run fast so the dark couldn't catch me. I tried to stay in the light.

No, this wasn't safe.

I turned the basement doorknob again. It twisted. I pushed, but nothing. It was blocked. Something big blocked the other side. I smashed my shoulder into the door but it didn't give. I was trapped, and had to go down.

Chapter Fifteen: Jervis Makes Plans

This house would do, but how to burn it? He looked about the room, and saw a bottle of 100-proof vodka. It sat on the table like a can of gasoline delivered from God. He would drink some and pour the rest on the curtains, on the walls, on the furniture, and watch it ignite.

He had lighters in his pocket. This place would burn. Firemen would come 30 minutes later and hose it down, not enough to save it for normal people, but enough for someone like him. Enough that others would abandon it and leave the house so he could come back.

The girl would be here, the ashes of her mother would be here, the man who burned down Oscar would go down—all of it. Jervis was master again. He would watch it burn from the street. He could find somewhere to stay for a few days, and then come back when everyone had gone. He'd return after check date, 3547, with money. A real master again in a new house abandoned by everyone. But he'd live here with all he knew—his girl in the basement, her mother in the tub, and his new family all here.

The refrigerator was held tight up against the basement door. After he had unplugged and moved it, even the cockroaches underneath knew it was time to go and scurried for safety. Now nobody could bust out of the basement.

He waited for the voices to come and tell him how bad he was. That he was a devil. They didn't. They can't get him here. Not when he was like this. He sat on the couch and started flicking the lighter. There was life in the flame. He held it against the side of the couch. The fabric burned, but didn't flame, only melted. The smell hit his nose and the smoke sizzled in his nostrils. He would use the vodka. Make it burn.

This was home now.

Chapter Sixteen: Lilly's Last Chapter

The basement seemed to echo. The basement seemed to breathe. Like I was inside someone's lungs and the walls went in and out, in and out, with each breath. My heart was racing and each heartbeat was faster than the last, like a drum solo that had to end soon.

Footsteps shuffled upstairs, then stopped. Was he really going to burn this place down? I tried to figure out what he was doing by the creaks of the wood. I would rather be in the fire upstairs than down here in this dungeon. I sat with my back to the wall with my legs curled up against me. The basement was quiet and frozen. I stared everything down for any hint that something might try to hurt me.

The furnace stood in the middle, with tubes that lead to secret places. I hated to hear it rattle. Every time I came down here I was terrified it would rattle. Usually it did not, but the few times it did it made me jump. Now it sat silently and mocked me, teased me. The washer and dryer stood by like two cold robots. In between were piles of clothes that lay unwashed, some for months. Stains of colored puddles were splattered on the concrete floor from leaks. Used syringes and tiny plastic caps from Uncle Nelson were nestled in a New Balance shoe box and then shoved in the corner as if hidden. A Lazy Boy chair with big rips sat in one corner, with broken curtains laid on top. A vacuum cleaner that didn't work but whined real loud stood upright. A ping-pong table with broken legs that stopped it from standing lay against the wall. My dad said he'd fix it for me but now the legs would certainly remain broken.

More footsteps upstairs. Floorboards creaked. The basement silence retreated. He was doing something. I needed help.

I went back to the top of the stairs. My feet clanged on the metal strips on the staircase and it hurt my ears. Nobody else could hear though, nobody at all knew I was here. I was too tired to scream.

I smelled smoke. Bits of it crept under the door crack. He was really doing this. Things were already starting to burn. Protective Services couldn't stop this.

I banged three times on the door with my fist and waited. Nothing. I pushed the door to see if it would budge. Nothing. I heard footsteps, voices, a muffled rant from the Red-Man talking to himself, humming even. I willed myself downstairs and then came back up with some towels that were old and moldy with mucky wetness. I tucked them under the door crack, but I could still smell smoke.

My house was on fire.

Maybe it will just burn on top of me. I could wait it out downstairs.

I went back down, the trace of smoke following me, and sat against the wall. My life was done, whatever happened here, and I already felt my body shrinking, my skin fading. I traced my fingertip along my veins of my underarm, from elbow to wrist. If only I had some H. The basement would seem beautiful instead of evil. Like Uncle Nelson said, *Until you have medicine to make you see the beauty, life is a sickness. A fucking curse.* But there was no H, there was nothing down here that can help. Nothing. Dad had a gun, but it was in his room.

There's always a way out if you just look in the right place. That's what the Red-Man had told me, but I had nothing.

Moments passed with only stillness inside, until slowly I was becoming part of the basement. The furnace accepted me as one who belonged there. The basement wasn't eating me, it was taking me in. I felt at home like I could stay here forever. I tried not to breathe so I could listen and hear every sound. All that came were drips.

Drip.

Pause.

Drip.

Pause.

The pipe from the upstairs bathtub was dripping, and each drip was bigger and faster than the last and making tiny splashes in the bucket. Blood and water that the bodies were soaking in was raining down.

Parts of all three of them—all of them dead in the tub. The image burned in my brain.

Grandma was dead, the witch of Brentwood, but her eyes were still open. Nobody could shut them for good.

And my dad, the one who cared for me, not real good, but he did the best he could with what he had. When he knew he messed up so bad that I'd be taken away he finally stopped lying. He brought me the skull of my mother. It seemed so grey and old and I could still picture the empty eye sockets. Mom had empty eye sockets. Looked at me with nothing inside of her.

I listened to the basement breathe and tried to get answers. I wanted to hear the voice of Oscar or my mom. When she spoke to me in my bedroom she said she was close by. I knew that to be true now. *Talk to me now when I need you.*

Drip. Drip.

The basement is all that spoke to me.

Smoke started to billow from the stairs. My vision became cloudy. It wasn't like hazy cigarette smoke but was thick, like chunks of oil were hidden inside. My lungs rejected the air and I was suffocating. This would end. It had to.

I walked over to the bucket and watched the red drips fall. The bottom was full of a layer of blood. Each drip made a *ding* sound on the metal when it landed.

I thought of spilling my own blood in the bucket somehow. My blood together with all of theirs would be victory. If only I could stick something inside my own defective heart and make it flow into the bucket.

Or if I could put them all into me.

I looked up at the leaky pipe. The place my dad would unscrew was loose but still attached. The pipe was too high to reach, so I pushed the washer over and pulled myself on top. I stood on it with shaky legs. Close to the ceiling the air was thick, steamy hot, and I held my breath as I turned the elbow on the pipe. One turn, two turns, three, four, and finally I twisted the elbow, exposed the pipe all the way, and soon it all spilled forth.

Blood and water from the bathtub flowed like a faucet. The red stream poured down the pipe, and started to fill the bucket. I held my breath for one moment longer while my unsteady legs got down from the washer. When I finally tried to breathe, smoky air filled my lungs and I coughed soot up my throat.

I knelt in front of the bucket as if peering into a pond, looking for my image.

A steady trickle from above made the pool ripple like the bottom of a waterfall. The bucket was a cauldron with a potion of red mixing and churning inside. Specks and chunks of grey were sprinkled in like little flakes. I tried but couldn't tell what parts of the blood were Grandma, what parts where my poppa, and what parts were my mom's dirty, scaly bones soaking inside.

I grabbed one of dad's t-shirts and cupped it over my mouth to help me breathe. It smelled like him. I liked that. It was all that stopped me from breathing in smoke. My eyes were full of tears from the smoke and the sadness of living my last days. The fire might stay upstairs, but the smoke wouldn't leave me alone down here.

I remembered the words of the Red-Man. Something he learned in a basement. *"We can shoot anything, not just the H. You're my girl."*

I rummaged through the New Balance shoe box. At least ten needles rattled inside, some of them old, some of them new. Any of them would do.

I grabbed one and held it in the air. Watched it twinkle in the light of the two bulbs that hung from the ceiling. Just then, the light bulbs blinked. Fast, then slow. Like they were ready to go out. I had to act. The house was going dark soon.

The needle was ready. I dipped it deep into the bucket, as if the best stuff was buried below the surface. Then I drew back on the plunger, slow but firm, getting in whatever would come out. Blood dripped from my fingertips as I pulled the needle up to eye level.

I wasn't sure what I was looking for, but I'd seen Nelson do this, I'd seen nurses do it for years, so I did the same. I flicked it with a finger the way they do, and watched the tube of speckled red squish in the needle. It was like poking at a fish tank. Things seemed alive in there.

The skin on my arm was so thin. I was just veins and bones. I aimed the tip of the needle into the fat of the blue vein. My fingers shook. My vein moved like a snake.

I felt the prick into my skin.

The warmth went right into my heart and spread up my spine into my head. Ahhhh, it flowed so sweet. It was like the metal syringe had tapped the base of my brain. My body was being filled, a hunger was fed deep inside of me, right into my soul's stomach.

The moment came and faded in a flash, and I had an incredible urge to put more in me. I became surrounded not just by smoke but by song, a whole chorus urging me on to use more, to keep plunging the syringe into the bucket, fill the chamber, and insert it into my skin. Blood from the bucket was spilling on my arm, but I did it again and again to get it inside of me. I could feel the new life pulsing through me, and saw it traveling through my body. My veins went from blue to purple, my heart expanded, beating against my chest like it was being filled with the contents of the universe with God inside.

Finally the moment came I have been waiting ten years for.

My heart burst in my chest. Blew open. That's all it could be, because a warm explosion blasted inside of me, like somebody shot me in the chest from the inside.

New sights flashed through my head. I had a vision of the Red-Man and felt him putting himself into Momma, injecting her with the sliver of metal years ago and the seed taking root and growing in her belly. I was dark in her womb even then, but feeding off Momma just the same. I felt my infant cries at birth from an ache that could never be soothed. I felt my dad putting a pillow over momma's head, holding it there—making it all black.

I felt Momma buried in the ground, trying to get into someone else's head to get me, her daughter, to safety.

I felt my daddy's strength, so many unspoken wars he'd been through, and my grandma's wisdom, who in her mind's eye could see the whole neighborhood and was always one move ahead.

And then I could feel the Red-Man, the person who started my life. He was watching my house from the street, and I spoke to him.

"You are an evil man," I said to him. "You're rotten and should kill yourself. Or I will kill you." I could feel the words twist and turn and roller coaster through his brain. He tried to block them out with rambles that weren't really words. Finally he mumbled back. "You die first. Better that way. If you kill me, then who will you have? Nobody. You are my girl."

"You are bad, rotten. Not a real dad, I'm not your girl. Get the gun and shoot yourself. Or come inside and cut yourself with a kitchen knife."

"My girl, you will be ashes soon, and we can talk then."

"Cut yourself. Again and again. With a big kitchen knife. I will make you do that. I will talk to you until you die."

I felt him pacing on the sidewalk, mumbling to himself, *then you will have nobody.. nobody. 3547, 3547.*

"No, somebody is coming for me. My momma tells me so."

Mommy didn't tell me I was safe as much as I could feel it. Flakes of Momma were in my veins and her warm hugs filled my insides. I was wise like Grandma, and strong like my dad, for their blood flowed inside me too. The Red-Man maybe had other voices in his head before, but none like mine. I would control him now. My heart exploded a new world of strength into me.

Black smoke filled my lungs and made my soul feel warm and black. There was no more coughing. No more tears. My skin was dark, thick, and magnificent. It was scaly armor, glowing black, not blue. My emptiness was filled for the first time. I walked up the stairs straight through the smoke and had its respect. The metal doorknob was hot enough on my hand to singe and burn my palm but I twisted it anyways, and I pushed the refrigerator away as if it was on wheels.

Upstairs was like a pool of hot ink, with only the glow of flames shining through. One wall burned and the fire grew as I watched. The blanket my dad used for a curtain was done, and the walls above flamed like a bonfire. The microwave was melted from the heat, but none of it hurt me. The flames embraced me, the smoke was in me, and I was in it. My insides were on fire, and would stay that way forever.

My energy spiraled inside of me, like a tornado that wanted to move. It needed to be spread to others. I wanted it in Joey, I wanted to save Oscar, I wanted to be in someone new, to carry on in them and be taken away from here.

But first the Red-Man needed to die.

"You're rotten. Come back inside the house and die with me. Burn by fire. Cut yourself by knife. You're a Devil. A Red Devil".

I waited in the house for him. Standing in the flames, I waited.

FINAL NOTE FROM THE AUTHOR - This story doesn't seem over just yet. I don't know what it needs, but something is left hanging. Some time on Brentwood is what I need for one last feel of the setting to close this story out proper.

I drive down Eight Mile Road past grocery stores, McDonalds, and storage units, and slowly the scenery changes to party shops, Baptist churches, and bus stops full of waiting people

My presence becomes more conspicuous with each mile I get closer, like an invading agent into a foreign body. Just seeing the street sign, "Brentwood" makes me smirk.

I remember the place from my visit as a social worker years ago, and it had changed only in that whatever was there 12 years before, was the same but now only more so.

I crept at ten miles per hour down the street, eyes casing the houses to spur my memory. The abandoned house that inspired the beginning of this story was indeed boarded up. Fresh planks were drilled over each window, and trash was sprayed around the outside like pinecones around an evergreen. It now seemed safe to walk by, but somber. The headstone of a man with a troubled life.

Across the street was where I imagined Lilly's house to be. And just as I had written, the house was recently on fire. Freshly burnt blackness from the flames inside had coated the siding.

I parked on the street next to a rusty blue escort, and when I slammed my car door, two girls who were playing turned their heads, knowing there was a stranger to this street visiting. Their mother was on the porch eyeing me as well. I don't think I looked like a cop, but perhaps like Protective Services come to visit.

I eyed the house from the curb. There wasn't a single glass pane left. All of them had been busted out. I've been in a house fire before, and I know that's what happens. Firemen with axes smash in every bit of glass, douse the house with water fast as they can, and leave the remains.

Standing on the sidewalk, I peered through the gaping holes looking for any movement, but saw nothing but darkness inside. I walked onto the porch, turned my head each way as if waiting to be invited inside, but then stepped through the front doorway.

I was greeted by thick, burnt air. It filled my lungs and searched each part of me, like a guard dog, smelling the visitor.

A man was in the front room. He didn't even notice me, didn't flinch at my arrival, but was pacing, three steps and a turn, three steps and a turn. His skin was an alien color, not exactly the Red-Man like I had thought, but perhaps crimson. His mouth mumbled words too softly and rapidly to hear, but they certainly had him in a trance.

At his side, his hand grasped a long steak knife.

He kept pacing, back and forth, and then raised the knife as if to strike. I crouched ready to flee, but before I needed to decide my next move, he put the knife to his own neck, and slid the blade along his jugular.

Nothing happened. No blood, nothing, just a groove in his colored skin that seemed deep as if it had been cut and sawed at more than once. Tendons of his neck were exposed, and his head had started to lean towards the damaged side.

On closer look, I noticed a liquid stain that ran from his neck down the side of his body, like he had spilled a shake. Blood had already been drained.

He took three steps, turned, took three more steps, turned, mumbled, and then slid the knife over the groove again. His head tilted, just a bit more. The cut was getting deeper and soon his head would topple off.

Walls of black, glass shards, displaced furniture, kitchen appliances broken or melted, all were littered about the house. I stepped through the wreckage and my footsteps made tiny echoes in the silence. I was at the doorway of the bathroom when I saw her. It was Lilly.

Her eyes looked up at me, brilliant bright white in contrast to the dark skin of armor that her flesh had become. Not flesh-colored black, but like the outside of a well done steak, leathery. It really was armor now, but she was more malnourished than I had ever imagined despite all my descriptions. I could have picked her up with one hand, and her legs and arms stuck to the side like twigs of a tree.

She knelt in front of the bathtub, as if genuflecting, waiting, but the tub was empty, it was just her, and the New Balance box of syringes at her side.

"Is the man still cutting himself?" she asked.

"That he is."

"He thought I would be his girl, but instead I am killing my father."

"He deserves it."

"You aren't protective service are you?"

"No," I answered. I wasn't even sure if my lips were moving, or if I was writing her words for her, or thinking them in my head. Either way, we were in full communion.

"But you are here for me, my momma told me so."

To that I had no answer.

"You are, I know it. You were here on this street before, and Momma used you. Got in your head and made you come to get me."

She said this and stared into the bath, which had a small, muddy pond inside. The liquid had turned black with ash and soot, but the bath was now empty of bodies. Still, she stared as if she could see someone.

I looked closer at her skin, which was full of tiny holes, most of them up her arms. As terrible a life as I had described, this was worse. I should not have resisted urges to hold back as I wrote. A lesson learned. I may have failed you.

Her hands started to rummage in the shoe box, and she held a syringe in her fist. Like a Hara-Kiri suicide, she pounded the needle into her heart, right through her sternum. It hit with a thud. If she gasped or if I gasped for her I could not tell, but I watched as she pulled the chamber on the syringe and sucked out parts of her own insides into the needle.

"You are here for me, my momma told me so, I'll be inside you. Take me away."

She had all the tenderness of a nurse when she grabbed my arm and turned it to its underside. Her fingers were still warm on mine, when I had expected cold, from this girl who I was pretty sure was dead or in some similar state.

When the needle went into my own vein, I thought of all the ways I had described this sensation, and wondered if I got it right. The pain of the needle itself was a sensual shock. It was a direct current to my spine, and quickly spread warmth to my whole body, starting in my back, shooting through my nerves, and finally into the tiniest capillaries of my brain. Tiny synapses soaked them in.

"Go."

I took a snapshot image in my head of this deadless girl, living in the ashes of this house, ashes of her family, ashes of this city. Her face was a mix of contentment and somber resignation.

I walked past the Red-Man who was pacing in the front room and slicing his neck with the steak knife every few steps. I realized I was leaving the tomb of both of them, and this house would have their presence here forever. I got into my car just a regular suburban drug addict, visiting the inner city and then driving home with the high of the drug inside of me, leaving the city dwellers behind.

I drove away with a hand on the wheel and an eye on the blue vein that extended from my wrist to my elbow. The vein was no longer blue but had become the shade of Lilly's black armor skin. My body burned with the buzz of her life and all that was in it. I indeed felt the rage and power of her dad, felt the sage of the grandmother, and the hopes and dreams of Lilly that could never be realized on this street.

And the love of her mother, Latrice. I felt that too.

But the feeling of Latrice was nothing new, and I understood what Lilly had been trying to tell me. The spirit of Latrice had been inside me for years. Ever since the day I visited the street for the in-home therapy session twelve years ago. Latrice had been nearby, buried in the ground, and she came into me at that moment when I had opened myself up to be spoken to. If only I had known what that burning inside of me was, the feeling I had confused for social worker empathy, that went from caring for the people on this street and turned into the urge to write this story.

Latrice was the puppet master who got inside heads, and I was the puppet.

And now I had Lilly inside me, Lilly's point of view, all of it burning through my veins, pumping through my heart, and part of me forever. I was taking her away from here, which is what Latrice wanted all along. I was the giant peach, and I needed to write about it, to catalogue it all best I could with meager skills but an eager heart. Obsessed I became at times to get this story down. Latrice commanded it so, and Lilly let me see through her eyes. To write her in the first person point of view.

So I did. We did. All of us. And that is the story that you have just finished reading. And now that it is done, there is this urge inside me to do the things that Lilly could not. An urge that comes from Lilly herself.

Joey from next door. I would watch over him as I could. I would do that, to be the peach that rescued him. As long as I believed in this kind of magic, I was sure to find it.

But not just that, there's more. I feel driven, obsessed even, to go to the house across the street. Lilly wants to me to visit the house were Oscar lived, the place he died in the smoke from her own dad's fire. She says she knows how to save him. She says she can bring him back.

I drive there on a Tuesday night and park my car on the street, which has now become familiar. With the claw of a hammer I pull back on the boards at 617 Brentwood. The wood plank resists at first, but soon starts to give, and the scent of the smoky air is released. I'm back inside...

Acknowledgments

I've had this story in my veins and spent many hours letting it bleed out. Being the spouse of one who has such an obsession is not always pleasant, so I owe a huge thanks to my wife and family. Thanks to Kealan Patrick Burke for making the cover shine and Richard Thomas for making the insides glisten. Both were a joy to work with. So many authors have given me support along the way, to name a few; John F.D. Taff, Julie Hutchins, Joe Hart, Peter Rosch, Shana Festa, Michele Miller, and Jan Kozlowski. Thanks to the beta-readers who helped shape this story including author Gary Cecelia and Charlene, Deborah, and Chris from Goodreads. Thanks to the millions who had a hand in my own sobriety, most who are unaware of how they helped. I will continue to drink in their milk-blood, and offer my own in time of need.

About the Author

Mark Matthews has worked in addiction and mental health treatment for nearly 20 years, and writing for just as long. His books are all based on true settings, including the horror novel, On the Lips of Children which is based on a predawn run on a dark San Diego trail. Like MILK-BLOOD, his novels STRAY and The Jade Rabbit are also set in Detroit. He is an avid runner, and has completed over a dozen marathons. He is a graduate of the University of Michigan, a licensed professional counselor, and lives near Detroit with his wife and 2 daughters. Reach him at **xmarkm@gmail.com**

Reviews are what keep authors breathing. Please consider leaving a few thoughts on Amazon.

ALSO BY THE AUTHOR

ON THE LIPS OF CHILDREN

"One of the scariest novels I've read all year." ~*The Horror News Network*

"Top Horror Read of 2013" ~*A Readers Review Blog*

"A dark, bloody book, at its bleak heart about the love a mother has for her children and the lengths she will go to for them to survive. You'll never look at jogging, the homeless, or even vampires the same way again. And, no, this book isn't about and doesn't feature vampires at all. What's featured here is infinitely worse." ~*John F.D. Taff, author of Little Deaths and The Bell Witch*

STRAY

""I loved this book! It was very believable & wonderfully written. Be ready for an intense read that will change your views on addiction." ~*Kandes Starlin, Book Reviews by Kandes*

"Stray is about addiction, yes. But mostly it is about relationships and the bonds that keep us all from going astray. Whether it's your wife or a hardscrabble mutt on the side of the highway, it's the connections to other creatures in the world that give us our forever homes. The writing here is clean, vivid, and wildly empathic to all the beasties who take shelter in communal spaces. Stray sings." ~*Sacha Scoblic, author of Unwasted: My Lush Sobriety*

"The characters are colorful and believable, and I was especially impressed by the author's realistic balance between the tragic despair and the very real hope of recovery that come with addiction. I recommend this book for anyone interested in an honest, unvarnished peek into addiction and recovery." ~*Ron S., The Spirit of Recovery*